Monkey in Resi

By Xu Xi

Published by Signal 8 Press

An imprint of Signal 8 Press Limited

Copyright 2022 Xu Xi (S Komala)

ISBN: 978-1-915531-00-1

Cover design: Cristian Checcanin

Signal 8 Press Limited

Truro, Cornwall

United Kingdom

Website: www.signal8press.com

TABLE OF CONTENTS

Acknowledgements

Earlier versions appeared in the following publications:

Where the World Unwrapped 拆開世界: *Looking Back at Hong Kong: an Anthology of Writing and Art,* ed. Nicolette Wong, Cart Noodles Press, The Chinese University of Hong Kong, Fall 2021.

Interview: *Usawa Literary Review,* India, Inaugural Issue 1, 2018; *Upstreet,* Richmond, Massachusetts, Issue 13, July 2017.

TST: *Crime Reads,* December 5, 2018; *Hong Kong Noir,* ed. Jason Ng & Susan Blumberg-Kason, Akashic Books, New York, 2018.

But for the Grace: *Don't Look Now: What We Wish We Hadn't Seen,* ed. Kristen Iversen & David Lazar, Ohio State University Press 21st Century Essay series, 2020.

Monkey in Residence: *The Darkling Halls of Ivy,* ed. Lawrence Block, Subterranean Press, May 2020.

A Brief History of *Deficit, Disquiet & Disbelief* by 飛蚊 **FeiMan**: *Speculative Nonfiction,* Issue 1, October, 2018.

The Youngest Child: *The Script Road,* Macau, 2018.

When Your City Vanishes, *Cincinnati Review,* University of Cincinnati, Ohio, Issue 18.2, Fall 2021.

Rhododendrons: *Jewish Noir II,* ed. Kenneth Wishnia & Chantelle Aimée Osman, PM Press, September, 2022.

背景 **The View from 2010**: *Massachusetts Review,* Amherst, 60th Anniversary Issue, Winter 2019.

Lightning: *The Culture Trip Original Fiction*, London, UK, Inaugural Issue, 8 November, 2018.

Winter Moon: *Still* (responses to photographs by Roeloef Baaker), ed. Nicholas Royle & Ros Sales, Negative Press, London, UK, September 2012.

Jazz Wife: *Eyescream*, Space Shower Network, Tokyo, Japan, December 2017 (Japanese translation); *The Jazz Fiction Anthology*, ed. Sascha Feinstein & David Rife, Indiana University Press, 2009; *Brilliant Corners*, Williamsport, Pennsylvania, Summer 2008, Vol. 12 No. 12; *The Story Hall*, Rain Tiger, April 2006. www.raintiger.com/storyhall/spotlight, *Tattoo Highway*, Hayward, California, Issue #6, 2003. www.tinamou2.com/th; *The Wild East*, Hong Kong, 2003.

I Had a Tiger Mom and My Love for Her Is: *Text: Journal of Writing & Writing Courses*, Australasian Association of Writing Programs, Australia, Vol. 17 No.2, Issue 18, October 2013.

For Alex Kuo

ONE

WHERE THE WORLD UNWRAPPED

拆開世界

W E were not truly native but we were resident. We were not expatriate but our passports were foreign. We were not temporary but we were not permanent. Only a few live in Hong Kong now, but we all look back at the city as home, because this was our city where the world once unwrapped all of our senses, the city whose qi still exhales a universe of dreams.

There could never have been a better childhood, we say on Zoom or via WhatsApp, now that international travel has been wrested from our lives since the advent of Covid. We were all girls there once, we part-Chinese, not-quite-Chinese, locally-born other, mixed-race or Eurasian, we Portuguese, English, Indian, Laotian, Malaysian, Indonesian, Danish, Spanish. We whose families arrived from many corners of the world. These days, we lose count.

In 2019 I answered the call, reluctantly at first, a little wary of this "old girls" network from my Catholic primary and secondary school in Kowloon. *French class 1970,* their WhatsApp moniker, recalled a summer of freedom, the year my Form V public exams were finally over and the future remained a blur of uncertainty. We were the French class girls, students classified as *non-Chinese enough* who were exempt from taking Chinese in our local, government-subsidized school. But French as a subject only began in Form 1. Before that students either took Chinese or were part of English "study group." I had done both, obediently slogging my way through Primary 4 Chinese until I finally admitted defeat.

Not a minute too soon because I would definitely have failed Chinese at the end of Primary 6 in the secondary school entrance exam. Alors, voilà: je suis, je serai, et nous sommes comme les étudiantes Français.

Mai Po Wetlands, New Territories, Hong Kong SAR and Shenzhen, PRC, February 2019 © Xu Xi

With few exceptions, it had been decades — over half a century — since I'd seen any of these women. Unlike the majority I had until very recently lived and worked in Hong Kong, and had split time between there and home in New York City for even longer over some twenty years. In the past decade, I was resident far more often in Hong Kong, where I paid annual income taxes, plus utilities, rates, and management fees for the family flat as well as monthly charges for my own local landline, broadband, and cellphone accounts. Some had left in the sixties, most by the seventies or the eighties at the latest, and did not have family to come back to visit, the way our Chinese classmates did. I was in touch with those classmates who returned to or remained in Hong Kong, and we regularly met the ones visiting from abroad. These were mostly *not* the French class girls, and over the years, my friendship grew with the ones rooted in the city, and conversations were more often Cantonese than English.

Among French class 1970, back when we were girls, we always saw the rest of the world as our future.

Yet, now — Post Umbrella Movement; post the subsequent unrest that rocked the city with protests, battles, barricades, firebombs, and tear gas, the likes of which we last saw in 1967; post a government crackdown so unexpectedly draconian in its repression of all freedoms we once took for granted — now we look back and wonder: will Hong Kong belong to our future, the way it belongs to our past?

§

Nostalgia can be tedious. One reason I initially resisted the idea of re-connection with French class 1970 was trepidation at nostalgic reminiscence about a place many of them no longer really knew. It's too easy to remember the good old days as good, and overlook what was wrong about the city, why we chose to leave, why we did not return more often than we could have. If not for my mother, whose Alzheimer's decided my return to live at home with her for almost eight years until she died, I probably would have been more like them. Making a life elsewhere — in Canada, Australia, the U.S. — countries where we mostly ended up, and personal choice would determine whether or not we flew "home" less or more often in the intervening half century.

Returning to Hong Kong is not a necessary journey if there are no parents who tug at our filial conscience or practical problems like family property that must be dealt with *back home*. If spouses, children, or lovers, as well as other family and friends beyond the South China Sea command our attention, why waste time and money flying back for just a little nostalgia? Among my Chinese schoolfriends *back home*, nostalgia reigns supreme at our gatherings. We shriek over the way we used to be, indulge in a past both privileged and pristine, celebrate memories to be preserved for ourselves alone. Our laughter peals through restaurants where other diners wonder if we've gone mad. Nostalgia offers us relief from our lives, to celebrate our lost youth, a time of bliss and self-discovery when the promise of tomorrow fueled dreams, before life and destiny prevailed.

Yet since removing my life from the city of my birth, the city that was still home until autumn of 2018, I am drawn towards strangely nostalgic quests. Months before French class 1970 claimed my attention, I had joined the Facebook group "Hong Kong in the '50s, '60s and '70s" to see images and memories from a colonial past. There are implied rules for this group: you need to be courteous and considerate, you must not promote your business or products, and, above all, you are not welcome if you wish to debate political or other issues of today, because this is all about a Hong Kong that no longer exists. Clear boundaries are reassuringly definitive. A "colony" is not independent or self-determined; there is separation between colonizer and colonized; all residents or "belongers" of the city are not created equal and we need not pretend to be. The group's membership comprises those who lived in the city during the '50s, '60s, '70s, and many are British. This slice of time ensures we share similar memories and can celebrate the city as it once was.

Would I reflect on the past with this hint of sentimentality if I had not been so privileged? Sentiment often arises from privilege, because rose-colored lenses readily prevail. It is not only about money and class — although these do play a significant role — because even poverty may be sentimentalized in a city where rags-to-riches, or at least lower-to-middle-class, is the journey for many. In a migrant city, populated in the fifties and sixties by those who fled a Communist rule that did not favor intellectuals, entrepreneurs, landlords, or those who clung to tradition, many arrived impoverished. They may have been rich in other ways, but even those who fled with gold and wealth had to start all over again in British Hong Kong as second-class, colonized citizens.

A Hong Kong Boomer, as I am, is readily dismissed by Millennials and younger as forever harking back to a past existence that is no longer relevant. After all, they never witnessed the kind of material deprivation or lack of access to education and opportunity, all the basics of 衣 食 住 行 available in the modern city for most people who now live well beyond sheer survival. The young are not wrong to think of us Boomers as "ancient history" when it comes to contemporary concerns.

But now the paranoia of passport immigration, reminiscent of both the sixties and eighties, is resurgent. Those Millennials and younger already blessed with a foreign passport have ways to detach themselves, even if they choose to protest and fight for democracy. Even those without a foreign passport have travelled, are well educated, will find their footing somehow, whether they remain or leave. I like to think they might now view their Boomer parents or grandparents as a tad less "ancient" or irrelevant.

§

Let's talk about privilege. Mine arose primarily from being a foreign local. My father's nouveaux riches gave me an extraordinarily special childhood, filled with parties, fancy dresses, expensive toys, foreign books and foods, and a little travel to Southeast Asia. Even Dad's bankruptcy when I was ten — he never amassed real wealth again — became a kind of privilege, because it forced me to examine the who, what, where, how, and why of my life. *I am what is around me,* begins Wallace Stevens's poem "Theory." For a writer, this surpasses manna, bequeathing you a spiritual room of your own.

My Hong Kong was where and how I first unwrapped the world. Not being entirely local, there was no stigma in embracing the English language as my own, because Chinese, or rather Cantonese, would never "belong" entirely to me. My parents' mother tongue was Javanese, and Dad was bilingual in Mandarin as well; English was for both their third language. But English was the language of power in colonial Hong Kong, at a time when a native-language fluency set me apart, notably, from locals. White faces never intimidated me because I talked back, and later, wrote back, to Empire. Ironically, this still hasn't changed, even though Cantonese and Mandarin are now both official languages as well, because at the dawn of the 21st century, English is the world's lingua franca for pretty much everything. Life, after all, *is* unfair. Yet in Hong Kong today, all but the ostriches know that Chinese, meaning Mandarin, could eventually become the city's lingua franca, and perhaps even the world's, sooner than perhaps many are willing to acknowledge. But that's probably the subject of another essay.

More important than mere English fluency, however, was my early appreciation for other languages, peoples, and cultures. Growing up in Tsimshatsui by the harbor meant I lived at the crossroads of the world. It was not unusual to hear a range of Indian, European, or Asian languages, spoken by residents and visitors in the district, and also at home. My parents brought many foreigners to our home, including relatives and friends from Indonesia, as well as my father's business associates: Japanese, English, Portuguese, Filipino, among others. Visitors to our home comprised a multi-culti mélange — mixed-race or transnational aunties and uncles whose global journeys touched down in Wales, Singapore, China, Indonesia, East and West Malaysia, Japan, the Philippines, Portugal, England, Canada, the United States, Australia, and elsewhere. At home, we always had a globe and an atlas to unlock the mysteries of foreign places.

My father's Mandarin fluency meant he spoke accented Cantonese, the way other non-Cantonese Chinese in the city did. Dad's long-time office partner was Shanghainese, and his Cantonese landed differently on my ear than the Cantonese I heard from the majority population. We ate at restaurants owned by Fujianese (or Fukkienese). I learned early on that I was not even *the right kind of Chinese for Hong Kong*, as my ancestors had found their way to Central Java from Fujian. Being Indonesian 華僑, I couldn't visit China on that passport until much later, unless I answered the Motherland's call in the sixties to 愛國, the way one of my uncles did. He died in Hong Kong a China patriot. Even though I disagreed with his unquestioning "nation love," my acceptance of it stemmed from an appreciation of China as something larger than merely the Communist Party. 愛國 or love for the nation was also about people, a way of life, and most of all, a way of being, of feeling you can belong in your own skin, without compromise to the West.

As a child, China terrified me, because we heard many reports about how bad it was under Mao, how persecuted some of my own relatives were, including my patriotic uncle who was relegated to a pig farm. But I also listened to those other Chinese voices, the non-Cantonese ones, whisper their alienation in Hong Kong. The Hong Kong Cantonese exhibited a different kind of persecution, cultural rather than political, and post-colonially, they became our overlords the way the British once were. My siblings and I, privileged by our local education to speak with a correct accent, mocked our parents' 走音 Cantonese. But their "run-tune" tones taught me not to close the door to languages, accents, cultures, and other ways of being "Chinese." In graduate school I studied Mandarin to recoup some literacy and to speak, albeit badly, this four-tone dialect-language, because China was, is, and will always be as much my world as the United States, a country I've chosen to also call home.

§

This adaptable and fluid way of being is something I've come to think of as *made in Hong Kong*. Had my parents moved to Hawaii when I was a young teen — that opportunity had presented itself to our family thanks to my mother's profession as a pharmacist — I would have become more culturally and linguistically constrained, given the monolingual and insular culture in the U.S. Looking back on the city now, I am struck by how cosmopolitan we all could be, regardless of background, ethnicity, class, or experience.

Let's jump ahead briefly to the present day in this search of lost time. Unlike Proust, I cannot dwell entirely in the past, even if it is comforting to celebrate the madeleine or, in my case, the custard tart (Hong Kong's, not Macau's), such remembrances are, in the end, merely self-indulgent. Instead, it is far more exciting, if enervating, to consider the extremely cosmopolitan creative outpourings from my city that continue, unstoppably, despite the changing political, social, cultural and linguistic landscape. Covid prevents me from flying back home, but artificially intelligent portals take me to M+, Videotage, the Fringe, in addition to the literary journals, festivals, readings, and publications where I can stay abreast of new writing and writers. Interaction with worldwide culture marks much of Hong Kong's artistic expression. Even its Chinese-ness is not a single idea, as a Hong Kong Chinese identity is intermingled with a multitude of sights, sounds, symphonies, and 世界's. True cosmopolitanism — beyond what a superficial, globe-trotting party crowd embraces — colors the city's soul.

M+, Tsimshatsui, February 2012 © Xu Xi

"City Streets" Central Market wall art, October 2012 © Xu Xi

What I know for sure is that I cannot keep up with everything because *Hong Kong is water*, to echo Bruce Lee's famous "be water." Some of the protestors in 2019, and even back in 2014, proclaimed this as a slogan, and virtual Hong Kong echoes this all over its AI-verse on more platforms than any one browser or cellphone can visit. What is less cited is the rest of Lee's monologue, that if you pour water into any vessel — cup, bottle, or teapot — it becomes that thing. We have poured water into the city for years because land was, and continues to be, reclaimed for housing, hotels, office buildings, roadways. Even our airport.

Water infuses all my memories of Hong Kong. The little river in Shatin my father hiked to with my sister and me. Bride's Pool where every secondary schoolgirl class wanted to picnic, partly for its romantic image. The Rambler Channel where I swam as a girl at the 19½-mile beach near Castle

Peak, and where, in my twenties, I kayaked around the 11-mile mark. The High Island Water Scheme, which the government designated for non-development, a few miles from my home in Tai Mong Tsai, a village beyond Sai Kung where I once lived. The nullah that stank on Waterloo Road outside my school. A salt-water, Olympic-length swimming pool that jutted into the harbor at North Point, with low and high diving boards. I jumped off that high board twice, but the second landing was a painful crash against the water's surface, ending further attempts. The beach at Lamma Island about an hour and a half's hike from the ferry pier that, one villager declared, was the cleanest water in all of Hong Kong. Upon finally arriving at that infamous beach with my friend from Taipei, both of us hot and sweaty, we dove, fully dressed, into the sea.

An aquatic world where the shape of water contoured our geography.

Central Reclamation, February 2011 © Xu Xi

Let's jump ahead briefly to the future. Bruce Lee also said, *Water can flow or it can crash*. The typhoons I lived through in the sixties and seventies were sometimes viciously destructive, but climate change meant that by the 2000s, I had to slosh constantly through the deluge of black rainstorms, downpours impervious to umbrellas. Rainstorms worse than typhoons for drowning the city. What does an "Umbrella Revolution" portend for the climatic ravages ahead?

How long can we be water before we, too, like the Yangtze, must overflow our banks?

Paterson Street, Causeway Bay, November 2014 © Xu Xi

§

Hong Kong is a giant gift, wrapped in tinsel or fancy paper, with ribbons, bows, and streamers, all bright and shiny. Unwrap it carefully, do not tear the paper, keep the edges sharply perfect, smooth out and flatten the sheet so that you understand its geometry. The box may be a cube or a rectangular cuboid, a sphere, cone, cylinder, or some other prismatic shape. European chocolate tins came in such shapes during my childhood, wrapped as Chinese New Year gifts. The same was true for nuts, candies, toffee, and other delicacies. Hong Kong had a sweet tooth and still does. Expensive high teas in five-star hotels and luxury shopping malls remain the way we let ourselves eat cake.

But what emerges from the past is the problem of dentists. Until I arrived at my American graduate school in the early eighties, I did not fully appreciate the technological advancements of dentistry. As a child, I used to get chocolate wafers after regular checkups from my Chinese, British-trained dentist who filled cavities with metal. At the open-air markets, I would gaze at gold teeth in the mouths of older hawkers, and wonder about eating gold. The idea of a gold tooth struck me as slightly horrific, but remains an image that is my Hong Kong. Later, in the Chinatowns of the world, I would see the same thing and understand my mother's oft-repeated phrase: *you can run with gold.*

The nineties was when I first noticed bad local teeth. In 1992, I returned to Hong Kong to live after a second life away in the U.S. By then a U.S. citizen, I also worked for an American company. Which meant that for the first time, I actually knew many Americans in Hong Kong and could compare and contrast them against local Chinese. You can't really do that from a distance, because the context is all wrong. Observing Americans in the city — quite different from the

British who were more rooted there — I was startled by the difference in teeth.

Hong Kong has abysmal teeth, and this is true among young, old, rich, poor, educated, uneducated. Having become accustomed to American dentists, who insist on regular cleanings and flossing, I looked for a U.S.-trained one back home. This proved harder to find than expected, because the majority had trained in Britain. One I found did my teeth cleaning himself, as there was no dental hygienist, which is standard in New York. He was rather morose about the prospects of his American qualifications, which appeared under-appreciated locally. Dental floss was also not always easy to locate, and whenever I returned to the U.S., I would purchase some to bring back. I also noticed British teeth, less pearly white and shapely compared to Americans. And of course, there was all that cake, and other sugary snacks that everyone seemed to consume constantly. I had thought Americans ate too much sweets, especially desserts, accounting for their rampant obesity. Eating too much was not the problem in Hong Kong, although a seriously tooth-decaying diet was prevalent.

However, eyes were a different matter, because all through the nineties, two thousands, and teens, it was Hong Kong that led the way for me. In New York, optical shops and even optometrists still tested vision with an eye chart, years after my Hong Kong optician could check vision with a machine that accurately calculated my prescription. I never paid for an eye exam, unlike in New York, as that cost was rolled into the new lenses ordered. I was nine when first prescribed glasses, and it was a huge relief to be able to see the blackboard clearly again. But for years, this struck me as a defect of being from Hong Kong, because so many locals were similarly myopic. Now I make all my glasses at the optical store in Tsimshatsui I've frequented forever. The one time I tried to have a pair made in the U.S., they could not get my prescription right even after two tries. Just prior to my permanent relocation to the U.S., I had Lasik surgery performed by an ophthalmologist who had been my secondary school classmate. It's all about perception and trust. From my perch, the U.S. still seems less advanced, and less safe than Hong Kong when it comes to eye surgery or general eye care. Post-surgery, what minimal prescription I have left still resides at my optician's, and a WhatsApp text will get me a new pair as needed, anytime, delivered by international courier.

"Eyes" Hong Kong, November 2014 © Xu Xi

§

Since time simply will not stand still, the Hong Kong government has recently decreed that RTHK must begin broadcasting the Chinese national anthem before their daily morning newscast. The news hit my morning inbox from the

Hong Kong Free Press. One French class 1970 member who has never left Hong Kong posted another news link to our group. My response: *I'm surprised it took so long.*

During my Brownie and Girl Guide days, from ages nine to sixteen, I resolutely stood at all public venues when "God Save the Queen" was played, particularly when I was in uniform. Lord and Lady Baden Powell, founders of the Boy Scouts and Girl Guides, were a large part of my colonial indoctrination. That patriotic ritual lost its lustre in cinemas, where the British anthem played at the end of every movie while all the audience ignored it and streamed out. Every 17th August, I sang "Indonesia Raya" to celebrate the country's independence day, and in French class, we learned "La Marseillaise."

But the patriotic tune that lingers from my old Hong Kong is one my Form Four French teacher, an elegant and gorgeous Indian lady who wore the most beautiful saris, taught us, the love song "J'attendrai[1]." The lyrics speak to a willingness to await "your return," *le jour et la nuit*, always, and, by implication, if death prevents this, the wait is eternal. The song was a big hit in France during World War II, the way "Lilli Marlene" and "We'll Meet Again" became wartime hits in Germany and Britain respectively because they too voiced that universal desire and yearning for love, at a time when the world is awry, mired in a sad uncertainty. Despite its French attributes, "J'attendrai" is of mongrel origins, borrowed as it is from a 1936 Italian song "Tornerai" which may have been inspired by a chorus from Puccini's "Madame Butterfly."

What does it mean to sing or stand for a national anthem? Old Hong Kong was not a good place to truly absorb

---

1 Lyrics to "J'attendrai" specific lyrics referred to in the text are bolded: J'attendrai / Le jour et le nuit / **J'attendrai, toujours** / Ton retour / J'attendrai / Car l'oiseau qui s'enfuit vient chercher l'oubli / Dans son nid / Le temps passe et court / En battant tristement / Dans mon cœur si lourd /Et pourtant / J'attendrai / **Ton retour**

patriotism or countenance national pride unless, perhaps, you were British and remained completely untouched by local culture in this colony where you temporarily resided. "God Save the Queen" was just another symbol of your nation, not to be interrogated or imagined from the perspective of the other. Life was not so clear cut for me and anthems were a puzzle. There were so many, some more melodious or stirring than others. The lyrics[2] also speak to such an odd sense of identity. Why did the queen have to be gracious, or happy for that matter? After all, didn't all crowned heads lie uneasily? Was Indonesia's independence, repeated insistently, its greatest victory? Is that why this motherland was embraced both body and soul? Did the French consider themselves children of a father, unlike Indonesia's mother-land? Was that why a call to arms was vital, to keep out all impurities of foreign blood?

However, youth is all about emotions, best captured in music that seeps through time from my Hong Kong. The melodies of these three anthems replay themselves whenever I gaze back at school days, while the lyrics are imperfectly recalled. Only now can I think about and essay

---

2 Specific lyrics in the three national anthems referred to in the text are bolded:
England: God save our **gracious** Queen / Long live our noble Queen / God save the Queen/ Send her victorious / **Happy** and glorious / Long to reign over us / God save the Queen.

Indonesia: Indonesia, tanah airku / Tanah tumpah darahku / Di sanalah, aku berdiri / Jadi pandu **ibuku** (motherland) / Indonesia, kebangsaanku / Bangsa dan tanah airku / Marilah kita berseru / Indonesia Bersatu! / Hiduplah tanahku, hiduplah negeriku / Bangsaku, rakyatku, semuanya/ Bangunlah **jiwanya** (soul), bangunlah **badannya** (body) / Untuk Indonesia Raya / Indonesia Raya, **merdeka**! **Merdeka** (freedom/ independence)! / Tanahku, negeriku yang kucinta / Indonesia Raya, **merdeka**! **Merdeka**! / Hiduplah Indonesia Raya!

France: Allons **enfants de la Patrie** (children of the patriarchy) / Le jour de gloire est arrivé ! / Contre nous de la tyrannie / L'étendard sanglat est levé, / / L'étendard sanglat est levé, / Entendez-vous dans les campagnes / Mugir ces féroces soldats ?/ Ils viennet jusque dans vos bras / Égorger vos fils, vos compagnes ! / **Aux armes** (take up arms), citoyens, / Formez vos bataillons, / Marchons, marchons !/ Qu'un **sang impur** (impure blood) / Abreuve nos sillons !

on the disparate language of such transnational patriotism. "J'attendrai," however, is another story. Both the music and lyrics never left my audio memory, alongside a visual image of our tall Indian teacher, standing in front of her French class of mongrel students, singing this love song. Somehow she, too, this former flight attendant, found her way to my city and became a part of its fabric, like the yards and yards of sari she wore. During one class, she taught us how to wrap a sari, and I was fascinated by this complex garb and her utter lack of inhibition. For the colony's annual speech and drama festival, she entered a group of us for choric recitation and chose T.S. Eliot's "Rhapsody on a Windy Night." She was a little like Muriel Spark's Miss Jean Brodie, the kind of teacher every teenage schoolgirl should encounter at least once. We all were just a tiny bit in love with her because how could you *not* fall in love with such a romantic and radical figure?

Years later, when I saw the musical *Cats*, I would recall that Eliot poem, adapted for its hit song "Memory."

What troubles me now is that teachers today may have less and less space to teach their young charges to think, to experience the new and unknown, to excite their imaginations by presenting them the world at large. A local teacher was fired for asking students to consider the question "what is freedom of speech?" My Hong Kong always looked outwards to the world, unafraid, willing to consider the many different ways of being. A global city should do that, shouldn't it?

So broadcast "The March of the Volunteers" on Hong Kong's public radio stations. After all the British played "God Save the Queen" every night when television signed off until that practice was eventually abandoned as irrelevant or perhaps, pointless. Teach today's schoolchildren to sing a rousing military anthem that echoes the history of revolutionary China. I emerged out of colonial Hong Kong unscathed and undamaged either by exposure to British colonial patriotism or by the shenanigans of my renegade, ethnic Indian, French class teacher.

Why shrink the possibilities of the citizens of any large city, especially in such a global world? Hong Kong's youth today are far more knowledgeable than I was about the rest of the world, thanks to education, travel, and technology. The city was, is and cannot help but be a "world city" because that has become its existential reality. The transnational patriotism on display by the protestors of 2019 — unfurling and waving multiple national flags, appealing for support from the rest of the world through multilingual messaging, even singing "God Save the Queen" as one of their more curiously conflicted activities — is born out of the similarly jumbled set of emotions I experienced as a girl. Youth is emotional but also intelligent, creative and intuitive. It will make up its own world city, regardless.

> *So the hand of a child, automatic,*
> *Slipped out and pocketed a toy that was running along the quay.*
> *I could see nothing behind that child's eye.*

From T.S. Eliot, "Rhapsody on a Windy Night"

§

Shadows at the Walled City Park, Kowloon City,
February 2011 © Xu Xi

Unwrap. Unveil, unleash, un-inhibit, the way Pandora once
unwrapped what is often referred to as her mythical "box." It
was actually a jar that should never have been opened. But
open it she did, as dictated by her raison d'etre, and "baneful
anxieties" flew out, scattering across the world. Only Hope, or
Elpis, remained, trapped inside, because Pandora replaced the
lid before it could escape.

Reflecting on my city now, Pandora offers some curious
parallels, this story that originates in an ancient Greek didactic
poem by Hesiod from 700 BC. She was born out of Zeus's
fury at Prometheus, who stole fire from the gods. *To make up
for the fire,* declares Zeus, *I will give them* (humans) *an evil
thing, in which they may all / take their delight in their hearts,*

embracing this evil thing of their own making.3 So he ordered the goddesses to fashion out of clay this beautiful woman, Pandora, a kind of warrior-android with her jar of evil, bent on causing havoc in the human realm. The goddess Hermes offers Pandora as a gift to Prometheus's brother Epimentheus, who receives her, despite Prometheus's many warnings *never* to accept any gifts from Zeus. The rest is the story of these baneful anxieties unleashed across the world when Pandora removes the lid.

It's a lesson in what happens when we don't pay attention to warnings that are loud and clear. Was it not clear, despite the Joint Declaration, our Basic Law, and all the British Government's mutterings, just who our new sovereign ruler would be? Did we really not know the patterns of China's governance since the CCP took power? An alarmist attitude, perhaps, back in 1997, but as the years unfurled, the warning sounds grew incrementally louder. By 2014, the year of the Umbrella Revolution, warnings from Beijing were not just loud, but very, very clear. Peaceful protests had simmered and boiled for far too long in the S.A.R., and when violence erupted in 2019, bringing the city to a standstill, all protest had to be crushed. Now, hope is trapped *within the unbreakable contours of the jar.4*

Pandora's character is also intriguing, because Zeus orders Hermes *to put inside her* (Pandora) *an intent that is doglike and a temperament that is stealthy.5* There's an odd contradiction in this *doglike* intent with *stealth*, reminiscent of the conflicted local leadership that purports to govern our semi-autonomous city in China. Pandora has no real agency. She is merely a cipher, android-like, commanded by an angry

---

3 Hesiod: *Works and Days* translated by Gregory Nagy. Lines 57 to 58 https://chs.harvard.edu/CHS/article/display/5290

4 *Ibid.* Line 96.

5 *Ibid.* Line 68.

god to be doggedly stubborn and stealthy in order to execute
his vengeance against Prometheus and all of mankind. For all
its cosmopolitanism, my city cannot ignore its Chinese origins
or its political history. China has borne the humiliation of
more than a century of foreign invaders, unequal treaties,
and Western overlords: of governance, culture, language, and
influence in the territory. A thirst for vengeance will ensure
that the government will never be so compromised again
by Hong Kong's removal from Beijing's control. Not, that
is, unless another revolution occurs, when Hong Kong, as
China once did, refuses to tolerate being 奴隸的人們[6] any
longer. Are Hong Kong people "enslaved"? Physically, no,
but increasingly, there are those who find their citizenship
compromised, constrained, commanded into silence.

Pandora is created as an "evil thing" humanity will embrace,
"randomly scattered," filling the world with *evils upon mortals /
silently — for Zeus had taken away their voice.*[7] Silence may be
golden, but not if voicelessness must be a virtue.

§

Are there no more presents to unwrap? Is Chinese New Year
over already? Is it time to go back to school already? To look
back on Hong Kong is to hear firecrackers at every corner, taste
the too-sweet candy, watch the mounds of 瓜子 demolished
as we cracked them between our teeth and left a litter of
empty black, red, and white melon shells. Chinese New Year,
or CNY, lingered more than Christmas, because Christmas
presents of toys or games or books soon lost their magic, but
new clothes bought for CNY had a greater longevity, as did
the 利是 (or 利事 / 市) money which Mum made me deposit
in my Hongkong and Shanghai Bank savings account. Of
course, even the bank has disappeared, replaced by HSBC, a

6 From the first line of "March of the Volunteers," China's national anthem. 起來!
不願做奴隸的人們!　Rise up! Those who will not be citizen-slaves!
7 *Ibid* Hesiod: Lines 103 to 104.

globally anonymous behemoth.

CNY of my childhood was all about fun and excitement, never fraught with family obligations or stress. Later, as a fresh grad working in Hong Kong of the seventies, I loved CNY because the city hushed, no one was at work, and an adult me no longer had obligations because this very Chinese tradition was not as important to our family. Those many public holidays became a good time to run or walk in the city, freed of traffic and people, when all shops, restaurants, and businesses were closed. Only in later years, when CNY turned much more commercial as traditions fell away, when shops and restaurants stayed open and tourists flocked to the city, did it became a time to avoid going out.

Silence in Hong Kong is rare, as are streets emptied of crowds, and March of 2013 remains memorable for this because of SARS. Visitors stopped coming and life shut down completely. I ran and walked the city then as well, luxuriating in the stillness. It felt good to be a "foreign local," to be someone who did not share the anxieties of the local locals, who shut down life to stay indoors, away from the city's streets. It felt grand to think that this could again be the livable city I once knew. It is Thanksgiving in the U.S. as I write this, and the streets of New York City are relatively silent as they have been for a long while. The week before, I had descended into unusually clean subway stations, rode uncrowded trains to empty museums, and wondered, *will it always take a pandemic to make my cities livable?*

Pandora also brought disease to the world, where previously there had been none. Or so the story goes.

Yet this Thanksgiving, an American holiday I've rarely celebrated in the past two decades because I was usually in Hong Kong, there is a tiny breath of hope, despite Pandora's jar. Even though the political opposition party has since vanished from Hong Kong's legislature in a mass-protest resignation, erasing the last official vestige of any democratic voice and representation. The city did not initially fall as badly victim to Covid the way New York did. SARS acculturated Hong Kong to donning masks as an excellent preventive measure, and an early lockdown — with extensive controls and tracing however annoying and difficult — is the smart way to combat an invisible disease. At our last Zoom, French class 1970 compared geographical notes on Covid-19. As one Hong Kong group member said, *it feels okay here.* Those of us in the U.S. were envious, wondering just how much longer we must live with this sad uncertainty. Since then, however, things have changed and the long isolation Hong Kong subsequently suffered due to its draconian Covid policies erased the envy.

For someone like me, Hong Kong may not belong to my future quite the way it does to my past. But the future, as we Hong Kongers call it, is the 未來, the yet-to-come, is that which remains unknown until it arrives. Once you unwrap the world you do not easily forget what it contains. Memory is currency, even if people, things and place are distant. To only look back with eyes wide shut does a disservice to our history, our culture, our way of being. Hong Kong will not disappear even if we do. The young can find their way through the maze of turmoil because their destiny demands that they must. I once found my way both out of and back into this city where I first discovered the world. They will too.

Before

T HINGS were still fine, despite the dreams, until she forgot her grandson's name. It happened on their weekly Zoom, when he was being his usual, adorably talkative self. She had been half-listening to his digressively long tale about a kindergarten classmate — *so like his grandpa Bing, whose oral discourses were legend among his students, "lullaby Prof" was a Rate-My-Prof quip that infuriated him* — when he declared, how silly of Kumar to say my name's impossible to pronounce! My name's easy to say, right Grandma? And she had stared at him, mute, unable to recall his name for ten whole seconds until Lana, her daughter-in-law, said, Nai-nai are you muted again?

After the call, she remained upset, almost dropped the coffee pot as she lifted it up to pour, caught it, but not before hot liquid flowed black on her right forearm. Just before they signed off, her son Jasper — *although he's forever Song to her, embarrassing him whenever she lets slip his baby nickname* — asked if anything was wrong and she'd told him she was doing fine everything was fine and to stop worrying about her being alone in New York because things were worse elsewhere and at least here, the grocery store was just across the street. But she wasn't fine, almost missed the call because Daylight Savings ended and she'd forgotten — *how was that possible she was always so religious about time differences for all her international work conference calls, even social calls to friends, so tiresome this time change why can't the U.S. drop it the way Hong Kong did forty, no, forty-one years ago* — it was this noisome pandemic, this tedious lockdown, yet there was Bing again, *hey you, no more squawking from your privileged perch.* What she most wanted right now was to be home, where it was twelve, no, thirteen hours ahead in the evening, having Sunday dinner with her son and his family, savoring Lana's delicious food and playing with her grandson Sheng (or Bartleby) and his sister Yu Chun (or Monica), already two, chattering almost as much as her brother. After dinner she'd go back to her flat next door — *so lucky her neighbor was selling just when Jasper was buying so convenient their being next door and Bing would really have liked Lana* — listen to a little music and the eleven o'clock news before a restfully dreamless sleep.

No, she mustn't squawk, she was extremely privileged, even if she was stranded in New York, it was temporary. At least this was still home, sort of, although the apartment was old it was centrally located, walking distance to every subway line on 14th Street, and it was all hers now, the mortgage long ago paid off, a space for her and her family. Once before, it was even a rent-free home for her son when he landed his first job in New York after his MBA at UST. As Song, *no, Jasper*, said, why come back to quarantine and waste money in a hotel? Yes, it made more sense to wait till things settled down, at least here she could prepare her own meals and had her own things in a comfortable enough space with her laptop and wifi and besides, there was Zoom now in addition to Skype, Google Meet, Facetime, WhatsApp, WeChat, and she could still talk to all her old school friends and former colleagues, even if they couldn't meet for yum chas or dinners. You know how to use all those platforms, Jasper said, so you can accommodate those who aren't as *techy* as you. The way he stretched that, tekkkk-yyy, made her laugh.

Even her recurring dream of the past fortnight — *not nightly but disturbingly recurrent* — was amusing, or had been at first. A lover, not anyone she knew from real life but in the dream this man was a lover. She was about to call out to him because he was headed the wrong way, his back to her, but could not remember his name. We just made love yesterday I've known him forever she'd say aloud to no one in particular, and then the panic, how could she possibly forget his name? It was absurd. In her dream she was much younger, around forty, still sexual. Each time, just as the lover turned into the street ahead when she, muted, couldn't stop him from going in the wrong direction, she would startle awake. The first time she woke, she was wet down there and would be subsequent times, but not always.

Two years earlier, she had turned sixty, retirement age at HKU's School of Business where she taught and provided career counseling. Come back to real life, all her friends in the private sector said. They had been surprised when she left her successful management career five years earlier for a significant pay cut as only an associate professor. You're still employable, it's silly the way universities force retirement so early, not even sixty-five when you can at least get long people benefits. Viola, one of her secondary schoolmates, had recast the clunky "senior citizen" as long people, punning on 長者, and it became another bit of her Chinglish. Bing would think that funny she told Viola the first time she said it and Viola, puzzled, asked, who's Bing? Embarrassed, she said, sorry, you didn't know about my late husband did you, because by the time she fully reconnected with all her Hong Kong schoolmates, several years after she went home to live and work, Bing was already dead, far too young at forty-six.

Yet here, now, in their former New York home, he might never have left her. She had met Bing in the summer of '83 when she visited New York. It was her first time in America. The plan, because she always used to have a plan, was to take her two-week annual leave to sightsee after completing her executive MBA classes at Harvard, since the air ticket and US visa were already paid for by her employer, DHL International. He wooed her relentlessly, this funny man who, despite his ABC-ness, spoke passably good Cantonese thanks to his late mother, a translator who worked with immigrants. The first time she described his mother's work as helping those most unfortunate ones, he frowned, *what do you mean, unfortunate?* and they almost got into an argument because she wouldn't back down from her position that being a Chinese migrant in any non-Chinese country marked you as lesser, making you one of the unfortunates, because no matter how hard you tried to assimilate you'd always be different, an outsider. Just semantics, she said, trying to soothe his irritation, because he raised his voice, *you have no idea, do you, what it's like to be someone who doesn't come from your kind of privilege!* He accused her of lacking empathy, something he prided himself on, and which he said she could learn by reading more literature. He was still in grad school at the time, completing his PhD in Asian-American Studies and books by Chinese-surnamed writers she'd never heard of littered his apartment.

Some of those books are still here, lining the solid oak, floor-to-ceiling bookcases that covers their home's entire west wall. Of course, it had taken her almost seven years of pestering him to replace his cheap, paste board shelves that buckled precariously, threatening collapse so that they'd both be buried under an avalanche of words. It's early morning as she sips her coffee and stands in the middle of the living room staring up, thinking, those top shelves probably need dusting, they must be filthy. Trying to recall the last time she'd read any book that wasn't a business textbook.

You should have stayed. His voice, like her tinnitus, sneaks up from behind, frightening her, and she turns her head fully expecting to see him. She wants to shout, stop hounding me, you're... but instead she collapses on the sofa and weeps, spilling her coffee. Between her legs, the memory of that dream makes her hornier this morning than she's been in years. As she cleans up the mess, the repetitive drone — he left me, he left me — and no matter what she does this morning, she can't stop crying.

By noon, she is calmer. Her daily tai chi exercise routine centers her, makes her less jittery. Lana says she drinks too much caffeine, which she'd dismissed at first, but after cutting her morning coffee with half decaf, and reducing the amount of tea she consumes daily, she does notice a difference. And the high pressure water jet in the shower reduces the tinnitus hum so she simply stays under the water roar a few seconds longer each morning. Mind over hearing, another Lana-ism, more health advice that her daughter-in-law, an exercise and health nut, constantly offers, unsolicited. Damn Lana, always so insistent, always so right. Just like Bing. She loves Lana, of course she does, the best wife for Jasper and a wonderful mother, and whose Cantonese improves noticeably every time they meet and whose Mandarin is more fluent than her son's. She knows she is lucky, *privileged,* as Bing reminded her constantly, to be who she is, to have what she has, surrounded by a family who loves her.

She has a ton of email as well as laundry. Focus on the practical, this has been her mantra for as long as she can recall. Those glorious early years with Bing here in New York, despite his precarious book shelves, are gone. Years where nothing mattered except being madly in love. The first time they made love is still astonishingly memorable. She buried that feeling for years after his death, trying *not* to recall because it was over, over, over and there was Song to take care of, a real life in Hong Kong to live and not the fairy tale of New York into which Bing had sucked her with his persistent love. Viola had been persistent too, wanting to know more about her husband. Viola was, is, a psychologist — the life of the spirit doesn't die, she says — and she must admit it's admirable how Viola donates her time to help women in prison now that she's retired from private practice, keeping her own spirit alive. Of course, Viola never married and doesn't have either elderly parents or children or grandchildren to think about, unlike her. Ba is so old he frightens her grandchildren, especially Yu Chung, and she's learned to keep him away from them since he can't remember who anyone is anyway. Sometimes, it astonishes her how hard her father clings to being alive — he's almost ninety — despite the complete loss of memory to Alzheimer's over the last twenty years. Luckily, she has Lily, a nurse from the Philippines, who is a wonderful caregiver and between Lily and Beth, her other domestic helper, she is freed of much of the day-to-day of looking after her father.

So why are you still so busy?

There is Bing again, haunting her, refusing to shut up, insisting on his presence in this apartment, his home. She can silence him in Hong Kong, because he only made it there a couple of times, the first to ask Ba for her hand, and only because she insisted. He had wanted to elope, expecting her to just stay on in New York with him, leaving behind her entire life in Hong Kong. To just *be his love / And we will all the pleasures prove.* He had recited Marvell to her, adding *I'll be…* but she cut him off, my passionate shepherd? How delighted he was that she knew the poem, one she studied in secondary school. Her teacher, Miss Lu, a romantic, had made her class recite that poem, one she was clearly enamored of. Who was her teacher's passionate shepherd, she had wondered, especially as Miss Lu never married, this attractive and stylish woman who taught at her school until she dropped dead suddenly one day right in the middle of class. Miss Lu was only thirty and she remembers how she and her schoolmates all grieved en masse, because everyone liked their sweet and elegant teacher. Luckily, she was no longer in Miss Lu's class when she died, as she told Bing when explaining why she knew this one poem. He hoped she knew other poems but she had to admit, no, she didn't and really never liked studying literature but that this one poem stuck.

She searches for it now, and there it is, on the Poetry Foundation's page. She had made Bing laugh because she also asked, what does that make me, your sheep? *You have,* he said, *a most American sense of humor,* which puzzled her then. Now, having worked for Americans and American companies long enough, she thought maybe she knew what he meant.

Mind over hearing.

Doing laundry calms her, as does cleaning the apartment. Living here with him had been constant housework-in-progress, Bing being rather lax about things. It took him days to go through his mail until one day, when she could stand it no longer, she gathered the pile, by then weeks old, and dumped it all in the trash. He was horrified, *but I haven't gone through the mail yet,* and she stared him down calmly, saying, and now you never will. After that, he was better about attending to his mail sooner.

But all this is long ago and so far away why must she recall it now? Ancient history. As Sheng said about her father, Grandma you're ancient, but Great Grandpa, he's fossilized. Lana tried to shush him but she laughed, said, well everyone gets fossilized sooner or later, which made Sheng laugh. Everything was fine until this stupid . . . *you can't blame Covid, you can't bury the truth. You should have stayed, we would have been okay, why didn't you trust me?*

And what about Song?

He would have been okay too, he would have adjusted. Just

boys being boys.

They were cruel. Stupid, ignorant, savage brats.

All that anger from before surges through her again. She is furious. Time heals nothing, all it does is passes by, unstoppably. Her poor boy, too slight and bookish at eleven to fend off the bullies. Suffering daily humiliation at the fancy private school Ba insisted on paying for because he knew she and Bing could not afford that on what they made, what with high American taxes and their mortgage. Bing was against private school, saying Song would do fine in public school the way he had, and become tougher, but she had gone to see the state of things, and had been horrified at the run down, decrepit condition of the schools and the unruly student mobs. It shamed her to have to ask for help from Ba, but her father had been so kind, said, you married a dreamer, he'll never be rich, but never mind, he's a good man. Ba also told her then, your mother would have liked him too. How angry Bing was when he found out what she'd done but she ignored his wrath because she knew she was right and that ended the argument as far as she was concerned.

An email pings. From Viola. We missed you last night, hope you're okay.

She completely forgot about this morning's Zoom with her former schoolmates!

Sorry, she lies, was tied up. Next time. But then wonders, what the hell, it's only four in the morning over there.

Why are you up?

Why sleep when there's so little time left, comes the reply.

It's only then she recalls that Viola lost her mother when she was still in school — hit by a bus or truck, something like that, as she was crossing the road to the market — and then her father died when she was in university — a blood clot in the brain — leaving her alone in their flat, the one she still lives in now, alone. Viola has no siblings, no other relatives in Hong Kong because her parents escaped from China by themselves as refugees who could never look back.

Like Bing.

The dryer tumbles to a stop. Shit. The mixed load has leaked red from something onto her favorite white T-shirt. *Separate, separate, separate, you're always so impatient.* Oh shut up you can't tell me what to do anymore. *Oh really? So why are you still back here?* Don't be difficult, but she is smiling. *See you're still my silly goose, aren't you?*

When she tried to defend her decision to go back to Hong Kong and take their son with her, one argument she used was that she missed roast goose. In Chinatown, there was really only duck. That made Bing furious. *You'd leave your husband and home for goose!? What's wrong with you?* Try as she would, she could not find the words for everything she felt. Homesickness, Song's well-being away from the bullies, air conditioning in summer (she hated Manhattan's stifling summers), higher salaries for senior line management positions, unlike in the U.S. where she would remain forever relegated to back room support — but all her reasons masked the real problem until finally, after their worst argument, the words tumbled out — I am sick and tired of being a second class citizen! It's different for you, this is your country. It isn't mine and never really will be, no matter how long I live here. He had gone silent, stared at her for an eternity. Saw her for real, perhaps for the first time. *Okay, I get it,* and after that there was no further argument.

It's already getting dark. She loves these autumn dusks, just as she used to love winters in New York. Soon, snowfall. Bing hated snow, because when he was a kid he had to shovel the sidewalk along his alley. Why can't the city do our street too, he'd demand and his father would yell at him to "collect his mouth," to shut up, and said that when he made his own money he could move to one of those ghost people streets the city cleaned because no one gives a fuck about Chinatown and yellow faces. By then, his mother was already dead — he lost her when he was seven — but, as he often said, he could always hear her singing, saying sweet things to him whenever his Ba yelled.

For her snow means silence. The city relaxes, breathes quietly until the thaw. Not like Hong Kong which is noisy all year long — the buses and taxis droned through all the nights and days of her childhood, and in the mornings, the clanging trams groaned past her flat, rattling the windows.

But it's still too early for snow and that silence she once longed for. The thing about dusk now is this tinnitus roar, which amplifies later in the day. Not always, but often enough, and here in an emptied out New York where the city has gone silent and she is always alone, it's deafening. Back home, the perpetual noise of the city masks it, she realizes, and the prospect of spending the winter alone in New York is troubling. This evening, panic sets in and she is not reassured when she reads about older people, dying alone in homes their families cannot visit. Stop, you're not that old yet, and your last checkup was fine. Stop worrying. She streams TV on her laptop and it's not till halfway through the evening news that she wonders why Bing has gone silent.

There are no ordinary days anymore. It's been almost five weeks since Daylight Savings — no, Eastern Daylight now — ended and still no return to normalcy. Outdoor dining as the weather gets colder is absurd. Besides, there's no one here left to call, no one to meet for lunch or dinner. She thinks about a couple of her former colleagues, but the two women with whom she was friendliest no longer live in Manhattan. One is in Seattle and the other is home caring for her elderly mother in Western Massachusetts. Zoom, Skype, Google Meet, Facetime, WhatsApp, WeChat, and more recently Signal as well are the spaces for meeting, the clingons to real life.

This morning, she is in the middle of answering an email when wifi vanishes. Just like that. She goes through the routine — unplug, wait, re-plug, reboot — but nothing. It's only Spectrum wifi in this apartment, no cable TV, so she can't even check if it's a system-wide breakdown. She calls the customer service line but is cycled through a series of auto responses that loop her right back to where she started until she finally gives up, hoping service will simply reappear, miraculously, now that AI rules life 天下 "under heaven" with an invisible wizard as emperor. The first time she watched *The Wizard of Oz* with Bing — a movie he religiously watched once a year and badgered her to join him until she finally gave in and agreed to watch what she called "this children's story" — she had been startled by how compelling it was, and how it made her think about China's dynastic history, emperors as the "sons of heaven" who ruled under the skies of the world that was 天. All of which had supposedly ended once Mao freed the country through communism. For the longest time, she had not understood why a children's story would have such resonance, especially one so foreign to her own upbringing.

Yet she recalls it now and suddenly wants to see it again, to bring Bing back. He has gone silent for days, more than a week, and she is confused, distraught, unsettled. Sometimes she wonders if she's going mad in this isolation. But she's not alone! She speaks to someone almost daily, at least five or so times a week. Song calls frequently, even Lana does, and there are the weekly Zooms with her family, as well as the fortnightly one with her old schoolfriends in Hong Kong. And former colleagues and people reach out to see if she'll do some consulting, or give a talk via Zoom. She is remembered, she isn't forgotten, even so far from home. Everyone assumes she'll be back eventually and all will be as it used to be.

She's mired now in the before time, in that long-long-ago time, the way her Ba is all the time, his memory unreliably reliable. She even misses sitting with him, listening to him talk about people long dead, people from his and Ma's youth whom she never knew. He will be ninety soon and she wants to go home to plan the celebratory dinner with all the family, his former business associates and the few surviving friends of his generation. Watching her father's memory deteriorate is a perpetual, existential shock, even though she should be used to it by now. Yet here, now, what she experiences is the shock of sexual desire, long stuffed away since Bing's death, along with years of entreaties by friends that she should consider dating again, perhaps even to re-marry, which she always politely ignored. There were always excuses: Song was only sixteen when Bing died; she worked long hours because she was a senior manager; there were the mortgages on the apartment in New York and the one in Hong Kong to pay, plus the New York one had to be rented out which ate up time; her Ba needed more assistance after he turned seventy and his mind wandered down that path of no return. Besides, when she looked around her world, none of her professional girlfriends who were either divorced or single were dating. As the only widow in her Hong Kong circle, she felt old, even at forty three. Plus she had begun menopause early. Her gynecologist suggested the shock of Bing's death might have contributed, but she has never been sure what to think and simply chose to believe that menopause signaled the end of her sexual life.

But back here in New York, her body in isolation is undergoing an involuntary transformation. Last night another dream, or rather, the next episode of her previous one sucked her into its pleasure tornado. She catches up with the lover and when he turns around it is Bing, masked. She begins to undress him and he resists at first but the dream cuts to the next scene, and they are both naked, having sex right there in the street in the multitude of ways Bing wanted to which she willingly used to succumb, and when she awoke, she was reaching for his torso to pull him back inside her again. The sheets were soaked with secretions and sweat and she was shocked by the musty assault. With wifi dead, there is nothing to distract her, and she recalls how she felt upon awakening, exhausted, after what must have been multiple orgasms that shot through her while in the clutches of a dream.

Surely this can't be normal. Perhaps she needs to consult Viola professionally, or ask for a referral to another psychologist. In the last few years, she and Viola have become closer, occasionally meeting by themselves for lunches, walks, concerts, or museum and gallery visits. They had not been close in school; her friends back then all became the bankers, financiers, tech entrepreneurs, management executives. None will leave Hong Kong, even those with foreign passports, although these days, their children might, and all are married to Chinese, except one, but that husband is an Italian who runs a successful business on the mainland and speaks better Mandarin than most locals and has declared he will apply for a Chinese passport. She doesn't know if he'll really go through with it. His wife has no intention of giving up her Italian one, or so she declared at dinner the last time they got together, and their four children and their families are all in either the UK or Europe.

She brews a strong pot of coffee, no decaf, just the real thing. It was all she and Bing drank back when she was not yet forty, when her body was supple and strong enough to orgasm away all those emotions she couldn't fathom. Like her

campaign to get him to apply for a university job in Hong
Kong, something he resisted until after she went home. "It
was so easy at the millennium, foreign talent was welcome,
especially overseas Chinese. What was wrong with you, why
couldn't you leave New York, even temporarily? We would
have been okay there, Ba liked you, and then we could have
moved back here together but…." She stops, realizing she's
spoken aloud. What is wrong with her? Why is everything
so difficult? The pandemic *will* end, besides it hasn't really
hurt her or her family all that much, they are the lucky ones,
cocooned. Clothed, fed, sheltered, vaccinated, and properly
masked, and who needs transport when there's nowhere to
go? Late spring and early summer was the worst of this year
but things are better now that it's fall and New York is ahead
of the curve with fewer cases every day. She might even be
able to go back for Christmas, or at the very latest by the new
Chinese year when this damnable rat year will finally be over
and the ox will enter the skies. By their calendar Ba will be
ninety. "Ba liked you," she repeats but Bing is silent and does
not say, the way he did on the eve of her departure back in '98,
that her Ba is a water monkey who will extinguish his own fire
monkey flames.

Her laptop belches and the wifi pops and whirrs again.
Some upgrade needs to be downloaded, Microsoft of course,
it infuriates her how often their software must be upgraded.
Song showed her how to turn off the auto update when
she complained about the inconvenience, grumbling that
programmers were so clueless about what customers need
until her grandson shut her up — but grandma programmers
make the world.

Both my husband and father are monkeys she had told
Viola over lunch, two days before she flew out of Hong Kong
in late February after the new year festivities ended. It was

to have been an easy, turnaround trip, three weeks, four max. She had been thinking to sell the apartment and planned to meet with realtors and pack personal effects to send home. Lana had even found her a moving company that handled small international shipments. Song is not attached to this apartment or New York, despite his time here, and Lana's family are all in Oregon or Russia or China.

Viola, who is serious about horoscopes and visits fortune tellers regularly said, how interesting, but what are you? She smiled, Earth dog the grounded one, and they both contemplated the exquisite symmetry of her life.

The quarantine rules in Hong Kong are ridiculous she exclaims when Song tells her the latest iteration. It's early December, and by now Lana is making noises about moving the family to Oregon because the government's latest machinations are becoming too much, even for her, this modern Chinese historian and daughter of American Communists who became more Chinese than most Chinese and who framed plausible arguments for Marxism and Maoism beyond the Cultural Revolution. Her wish to leave Hong Kong is the cause of much friction between the couple, she knows, even though they both put on smiling faces for her on Zoom. Song is, like her, apolitical. All he wants is to bring up his children where he feels most at home and where he can make a good life. After Song outlines all her travel and quarantine alternatives he surprises her by asking, how did *you* decide, Ma, to leave New York? He's never asked, never wanted to talk about it. She assumed it was because he had been so grateful to get out of that school and had fit easily and well into his new school in Hong Kong, an international one, where nerds were admired and did not need to contemplate revenge.

Before she can respond he adds, but you'll stay, won't you

Ma? For Grandpa?

Afterwards, she wonders if she's made the right decision to hold onto the New York apartment, even though the Covid situation will likely progress to the point where she'll no longer need it as a place to stay. Song didn't react when she told him this. Many of her friends back home say the politics are ignorable, not unlike the way it was under the British. What democracy did we have then, demands Melinda, the wealthy entrepreneur who made her fortune in Chinese utilities; her husband is a Beijing man. Melinda is the only one of their cohort who, as Viola says, married correctly into our future. Viola is much more ambivalent and privately tells her she holds a British National Overseas BNO passport which she elected years ago even though everyone said it was a pointless colonial compromise. It was such a neutral decision before, like a multiple choice exam where you might as well try to guess the right answer if you really don't know. The Hong Kong Government declares the BNO will eventually not be recognized, and she will be forced to exchange it for the Special Administrative Region SAR one, assuming, of course, Beijing continues to allow this exception for Hong Kong. Right now, if she wants, Viola can register with her BNO to migrate to Britain under the UK's special arrangement that so infuriates Beijing. She did attend a UK university, and has some friends and professional contacts there, but her real life has been all about Hong Kong and Viola can't imagine growing old and dying abroad.

Tonight she has episode four of the dream — three was so pornographic she refuses to replay it — and just like two and and three, she wakes up knowing that the orgasms have made her sleep more soundly than she's slept in years. The way sleep used to be with Bing.

All through October and November, she has tried to

record her nocturnal episodes — she began thinking of them as journeys through the city because each dream starts with following the lover. The street corners change, sometimes it's their own neighborhood, sometimes Midtown or Wall Street, sometimes around the UN or even Brooklyn Heights, and often the meat market district (when there still were markets), the Village and Upper West side. All the spaces she and Bing haunted. She has a log of all the episodes she can recall, hoping to make sense of this nonsense. What information she finds online about involuntary or sleep orgasms is sketchy. Regardless, what she is certain of is that Bing is no longer here. It's baffling. She is still too embarrassed to say anything to Viola, holding back because for as long as she's known Viola, she's never heard mention of a lover, either male or female. In fact, one of her former classmates, the one married to the Italian and who speaks openly about sex, once wondered aloud if Viola was simply asexual. It dawns on her now — the way so much, way *too* much dawns during this enforced solitude and silence — that she's rarely had a conversation about her sex life with any of her Hong Kong women friends, that the only such conversations were with Americans, the women friends she made when she lived and worked here, or the odd European or British expat in her Hong Kong hiking group, and how liberating that used to make her feel. When these women envied her her excellent sex life with Bing, she smiled, gratified at her privilege. Viola once mentioned that most of her clients, when she still had a private practice, were foreigners or hyphenated Chinese, the alphabet BC's from around the world, alienated in Hong Kong and China where everyone looked, and even sounded, like them, but shuttered them out of their worlds.

This afternoon, the super stops by to adjust her heating system. A new boiler for the building was installed this summer which is supposed to be quieter and more energy efficient. From the time she moved into Bing's apartment, Alberto has been the super. He's from Colombia and is getting too old for this work, he says, as they exchange friendly words. His son will take over his job soon. She's forgotten about his son, the boy who was about Song's age and the two used to play together until she realized Song was swearing in Spanish and put a stop to that. They're just boys, Bing had said at the time, upset that she cut off their friendship, but she disagreed, saying, Song needs a better class of friends. But now, as she chats with Alberto, this man she's relied on for years, she recognizes how horribly elitist that was, which was what Bing accused her of, and she is ashamed of the way she used to be.

In fact, as she prepares dinner that evening, and tries to construct a conversation with Viola about perhaps entering therapy (although the idea still frightens her), she says to Bing, "you were right, Hong Kong misshaped me." An echo from a hideous argument. It was the year after she left New York and Bing had come to visit, having reluctantly agreed to meet with the interview committee at one of the local government universities. They were hiring for a full professor position, with tenure, and paid more than he'd ever made at the university in New York where he'd taught for decades. When the job was offered to him, he turned it down, much to her annoyance, because she had arranged the whole thing through a highly influential friend. You embarrassed me, she told him, made me lose face. Face, he retorted, means shit without morality. *How* he harangued her about the inequities of what he called a lopsided postcolonial legacy and the elitism it bred, to which she argued back — and academia in New York is so great, where highly qualified, dedicated professionals are either adjuncts or on contracts like yours for shit pay — because his position had to be renewed every two years. Is that system any better than ours in Hong Kong?

"I'm sorry," she says to the skies. "I was wrong and you were right, so right. Look at the mess we're in now."

It's too late to make amends, which she had tried to do after the Umbrella Revolution, a democracy movement that rattled and unnerved her, by leaving her business career for an academic one, hoping to be of some use to the next, disillusioned generation. Bing would have approved, Bing who preached ending capitalism in favor of socialism for the 21st century. *Silly goose, silly goose.* She was happy before, why hadn't she simply rolled with that? Even Ba said, many times, my daughter he's a good man, your mother would have been proud of you, although she knew how it pleased him to have her home, a good filial daughter. Has she harmed her son with her brand of parenting? But Song seems so balanced and sensible and, well, okay. Besides, Bing would have loved Lana, they're rather alike, and that's worth something, knowing this with such certainty. Things have simply turned out the way they have and there's nothing she can do about it now, not about her son and his family who must make their own decisions, or the way Hong Kong is becoming, will become. There is no right answer to the choices presented by Fate. Besides, there's Ba and she will remain by his side in Hong Kong until he dies, which will not happen for another dozen years, when he makes it to over a hundred.

Interview

for Dad

THAT summer, we listened to every recording of the Concerto in D we could get our hands on. There was this slightly scratched LP of the Rabin at the library. Despite the skip – at the worst possible point in the Adagio – we all agreed Rabin's was The One. Cal tried to disagree, but Kent and I won that round because it was clear that Cal was just being contrary, and not calling the shots as he liked to think he did.

If you're asking me now did I ever think then that one day there'd be no Kent, and only a *smorzando* Cal, and that I would become this star Paganini soloist, I have to say no, not really. The thought didn't cross my mind. My life as an artist in the world now feels like the only one I've ever known. Back then, we were just three greenhorns in The Academy: Kent the bassist and well, you know about Cal. In bed, Kent and I only talked about Cal – *yes, sad* – and we were both positively, absolutely certain Cal would end up where I did. I even said I'd be happy with an orchestral career, because Kent and I became lovers only because we neither one could be Cal's. Not that we would have admitted it at the time. The real reason Kent is dead is less about AIDS and more about who he couldn't be. Kent wasn't promiscuous by nature, but he took Cal's dismissal much harder than I did and that destroyed him. The day after Cal dismissed us, Kent gave up pretending to be bisexual – well, he did sleep with me after all – and then, well, he didn't even show up to studio anymore and fucked so many guys we lost count. Late seventies. We didn't know about AIDS, you know?

How badly was I in love with Cal? Badly enough, but not so badly that I took to heart his dismissal of Kent and myself as artists. He was just jealous when he found out we were lovers. Yes, I know I said we only were because we couldn't be Cal's lover, but Cal was complicated, as you obviously must know, if you've been researching his life and work as long as you say you have. Cal needed us both to worship him completely.

Right, the Rabin. Cal dismissed everything else until we heard the Rabin. I was obsessed with Paganini – what violinist isn't? – and was exceptionally so because of my late aunt's obsession. Yes, yes, the music teacher aunt back home in Malaysia who adopted me, paid for my studies and life. You know more than enough about my background by now, the parents who abandoned me because I was a freak, etc., but anyway, we're here to talk about Cal, not me, right? Heroin, you say? Overdose? I'm surprised. Drink, yes, drugs, not in a million years I wouldn't have thought. Oh, maybe a little weed, nothing more. We drank, Cal and Kent and I. Every bartender in Manhattan knew Cal by name because he tipped a bundle. Bought most of our rounds too which burned Kent who was from some farm in South Dakota, and dead broke. It was easier for me being "the girl." What does it matter if I ever slept with Cal, you don't really want to know that, do you? No, I will not answer the question because it's impertinent. And unnecessary. You write your biography, god knows why you are, but I won't contribute to more gossip. You don't believe Cal was asexual? Well, that's your choice. I can't tell you for sure because Cal hasn't been in my orbit for a very long while, but trust me, I'm 98.9999% certain he's asexual. Of course I know he wanted to fuck me, eventually, everyone did, just to know what it would be like, which was why he was so jealous of Kent who simply took me at face value. I think that's why Kent was…. what was that? I'm the only violinist who knew Cal who'll talk to you? Are you really surprised? The man was a monster. Brilliant maybe, but a monster. He destroyed more careers than he nurtured, and I know all those evil, unforgivable things he said about me, telling the world what I am, which was humiliating, horrible. Heartbreaking. It was such a breach of trust. He knew I wasn't ready for disclosure then. But what I did know, even back then, was that he couldn't rein me in, even though he came pretty close. His betrayal ensured he never would.

It was all about reining. He had this trick with the bow. I hear it became his teaching method – what's that twittering thing everyone says now, hash tag? – his tag I suppose. It made me laugh but intimidated Kent. He'd sneak in behind you in the practice room and you'd never hear him enter. Right in the middle of the trickiest passage, the one he knew you were having trouble with, he'd stick his bow right across the bridge and whisper in your ear, *you suck*. I'm right, aren't I, except that he did it to his students to their face. And then groped. *Suck, grope, suck, grope.* Good syncopation. He destroyed himself as a teacher in the academy, but heroin, I have no idea where that came from. Yes, yes, of course that's how Cal found out, he groped me too. We were young. Oversexed. The young are always oversexed and live below the belt.

Right, about the Rabin. Kent looked a little like a young Michael Rabin. That high Paganini forehead. Like those early Sherlock Holmes illustrations before actors shanghaied the face. Kent was sweet. Look, I have this photo of the two of us, didn't he have a kind face? Bassists are sweet, they give strings a good name. Not like violinists.

A photo of Cal? No, none. He hated being photographed. His family's all gone, that's why you can't find anyone, and there weren't a lot of other relatives, I don't believe. He was still marginally in my orbit when his parents and sister died. I even called to offer condolences. You know what he said? No one will write their obituaries. Can you imagine that? I mean, I knew there was no love lost, etc., that he burned through his trust fund, etc., that his sister once tried to strangle him, etc. I mean I know they were all kind of mad, Mayflower shreds he called them. Made me think of that poem about petals and black boughs, you know the one I mean? However bad things got with my parents, I would never, ever say such a thing. It wasn't their fault they didn't know music. All they saw was this monster, despite my talent. What was it Jesus said on the cross? *For they know not what they do?* Cal must have been a horrible child. I'm sure he always knew exactly what he was doing. He told me once that when his sister was thirteen – she was a couple of years older than him I think – he snuck into her bedroom one night and cut off her hair. Right down to the roots. Claimed he was inspired by some Fitzgerald short story? Do you wonder she tried to strangle him? I'm sure he burned through what remaining fortune he inherited. You know, it was whispered he started the fire and locked them all in? I wouldn't have put it past him, for the inheritance, I mean.

Why am I telling you all these things about him? You're the one who's asking and writing this silly, silly book, when Darling, you know you could be doing one about me instead. That will sell. No one wants to know about Cal anymore.

Right, the Rabin record incident. He broke the LP in half. Kent was horrified, said, *the library will fine me* because it had been his turn to borrow. We took turns and kept the album out with us constantly. We were young. Petulant. The young are always petulant and mad about power and lust. Anyway, Cal laughed at Kent, called him a cowardly hick or something equally obnoxious. He was drunk, and we had just told him about us. Then, Cal slapped my face and Kent hit him, and there I was, two boys fighting over me, and oh, I can tell you it was exhilarating. Glorious. Laughable, don't you think? Cal threatened to amputate Kent's left hand. *Some night, when you least expect it,* and then he opened this cupboard and wouldn't you know he actually owned a surgical saw. Kent was terrified. I admit I was too, even though I tried to fluff things over, laugh it off. Etc. Be the girl. But then, Cal said Kent and I were no-talent wannabes, and that all we'd ever be good enough for was Mantovani's orchestra, and maybe not even that. That we had no soul, were not artists, that we didn't know how lucky we were he spent any time with us because *he* was headed for greatness and we were privileged to catch a little stardust, nothing else.

So childish, don't you think?

Whose idea was it to tell Cal about us? I don't know, I might have said something to Kent. Kent was terrified of Cal finding out so I think I just wanted to come clean. I adored Kent.

That's not what Kent's brother says? What does that ignoramus say, I never did like the guy. He really was the hick. At the funeral, he said I killed Kent. Murdered him. Can you imagine? Said Kent was devastated by my breaking up with him and would never otherwise have committed suicide. What a joke. Kent died of AIDS, we all know that. And he was gay, dumped me, even though I was the reason he could finally come out. Is that my fault? Don't listen to that loser of a brother. He doesn't know anything.

Cal says Kent didn't die of AIDS? Is he serious? Cal just can't admit Kent was in love with him he's such a homophobe. Look, if you're going to write a bunch of lies, this interview is over. I agreed to talk about Cal. Kent's history. You writers are *all* the same. Those who can't fuck, write.

I am not shouting.

Okay, that's more like it. I don't like going so far off topic.

Why did Cal have such power over us? Let me think about that a minute, can you? All these questions, honestly. They're giving me a headache.

Okay, so I suppose we were his first acolytes, masochistic enough to worship him. All megalomaniacs do that somehow, draw people to them who scrape and fawn and suck in the air they breathe. The bullies in the sandbox. The leaders of cults. The dictators who commit genocide. You're either victim or slave if you end up in their orbit. Nothing in between unless you manage to escape.

Time for cocktails, yes? I'll have Marianna make us some.

Okay, so I know Cal got this brief bump in the ratings because of Jezebella Oh. Another Asian chick with a bow and a schtick. At her last concert, you could see right through her dress I swear she wasn't wearing underwear. What do you mean the photo that went viral was doctored? Who could be bothered to do such a thing? I'm sure she's frigid as the Antarctic because she orgasms all over the strings, can't you hear? So melodramatic. And Jezebella! Did he name her that? What did he do, keep her chained in his apartment? They say he found her in the hotel bars, hooking. She won't last. His puppets never do and the word is she's with that Johnny-come-lately conductor in Ohio so she's already left Cal.

Did I *ever study with Cal?* Are you insane? Would I still be here if I had? Every one of his supernovas burnt out fast, you know that. It was a kind of talent Cal had, I guess, to prep them, dress them, prop them up and then toss them onto the pyre. Brides for Paganini. So Jezebella was the last, the widow.

Are you serious? She had a miscarriage? What did he do, impale her that fucking stallion? No I will not tell you if I slept with him, what does it matter? Yes, of course I've seen him naked. Before Kent and I started fucking we'd do these naked picnics up at Cal's lake house while blasting the Rabin on that portable gramophone of his. Oh, Cal had *everything!* An Aston Martin like Bond's. Champagne buckets he brought everywhere filled with two bottles. A platinum cigarette holder, you know the one, in all those photographs of me from those days? He sent me ten dozen white roses for my first Academy recital with a note that said, *hear you again in a decade*. Of course, a decade later we weren't on speaking terms and Kent was dead. And I already had my first recording. It still sells, you know.

What do you mean he's still doing his Brides of Paganini series? Cal's finished, especially if he's on heroin. Oh, he's not on heroin anymore? I thought you said… oh that was five years ago? You told me? Really? When? I'm sure I don't recall.

Yes, he gave me the Stradivarius. How? Had it delivered. It was shortly after my Berlin performance, the one about which you wrote that lovely, lovely review. So honest. It was the day the Wall came down and I was watching the news on television and the doorbell rings and it's this messenger service with the box and a single white rose. No message. Of course it was him, besides I recognized the Stradivarius right away as his. He'd already stopped performing by then, hell, he was too drunk and missed more appearances than he made. No, I didn't know he made it through AA. Good for him, I guess. What do you mean don't I care? He doesn't let anyone care, does he? Did he ask you to tell me that?

He told you I was Paganini's best concubine? What is he, the pimp?

Did I love *Kent?* What kind of question is that? Kent and I were – what is it the young all say now – fuck buddies? We were young. Ignited. The young are always ignited, desperate to explode. The trouble with Cal was that he was always putting a flame to our desperation. He grabbed Kent's bass once, in the midst of one of our endless arguments, put his fist against its back, and threatened to punch a hole in it unless I sucked Kent's cock in front of him. What did I do? I sucked Kent off, of course, and the next thing we knew Cal was coming all over the bass and you should have heard Kent shriek. Next to him, a banshee was *sotto voce*.

The last time I saw Cal? To be perfectly honest, I don't remember. One of his last concerts probably, which would have been years ago. Yes, I went to his concerts and no, of course he didn't know. The man had talent. Once upon a time, he had more than mere talent, he occupied that indefinable space between the angels and us. Okay, maybe devils, not angels. But that's almost too clichéd for Cal, like it was for Paganini. Devils were angels once, and the rest of us, we're just human.

Cal says we met last year? He's delusional. I haven't seen him for years. Decades.

Who was I to Cal? Darling, surely you know the answer to that one. I'm the one who got away. No, there's not much more to say about that. I got away. Let me repeat that. I got away. No, it's not true I once tried to sever his hand. Surely you don't believe his lies? The man is a monster and he'll say anything to make himself seem like some misunderstood genius. It is not true I broke Kent's heart, is that what Cal says? No, I did not try to seduce Cal, is that also what he says? Is that why you keep asking me all these silly questions? Darling, you know me. You've interviewed me, what, at least half a dozen times by now. I mean that's why I said I'd talk to you about Cal for your book, even though it's such a pointless thing to be writing, you do know that, don't you? It is time to set the record straight, to refute all those lies he's told about me, not that anyone has listened to him for a long, long while.

Come on, be honest. I won't tell. You're not *really* writing a book about him, are you?

Darling? You've gone awfully quiet. Marianna makes a mean martini, don't you think? Come, come, stop pouting. I didn't mean what I said about writers and fucking. You know me, I'm not really mean, not like Cal.

Last thoughts? Are you leaving already? Marianna can make us more cocktails, and if you like, I'll order some food from that great Italian trattoria round the corner, you know the one. You're having dinner with Cal? Does the man still eat? I've heard tell he's a wraith of his former self.

Oh, you're bringing him dinner. What are you, his butler?

Now, now, don't be petulant, we're all too old for that by now. Okay, last thoughts, if that's what you insist.

Hang on, I'm thinking. I do think, you know.

The Concerto. Paganini meant for it to be heard in E flat, not D, as I'm sure you know. It's the difference between genius and terror. Cal's no devil, any more than Paganini was. They're both just terrified, except that Paganini was extraordinary, while Cal, well Cal just gave into the terror. No one will write his obituary but they will write mine.

You make sure you tell him that.

T S T

LISTEN *to me, it's not too late.* On quiet nights, you will hear us speak. At the end of the last water snake year, the year that *autre* calendar brackets between February 10, 2013 and January 30, 2014, our storytelling began. During that lunar year, **Seven Sisters Club** vanished for good. Once upon a time, a perfect geometry of white smoke against dark pistachio and rust that was almost vermilion graced its façade. Remnant tiles, like torn evening wear, barely cover the gunmetal wall now, but under streetlight, the colors still glow. I watched the building disappear. Each year, a little more deterioration — a sign gone, a door off its hinges, a window pane shattered — until finally, the wreckers appeared and now, we might never have existed at all.

The girls, they were all there, most idling in doorways along **Minden Row**, others squatting along the uphill path towards what had been the Royal Observatory, some loitering at the crest of the hump towards Middle Road. They all came to tell their stories to anyone who would listen, and once they started, they wouldn't shut up.

But the first time they came it was because I called. Our home was gone and we needed a way to come together. We were like that, you see, undeniably sisters in eternity's muddle. The Milky Way swirled through our story every 乞巧節, that Chinese heavenly Romeo & Juliet story for thwarted lovers all girls adore. Occasionally, we gathered in the forgotten village in North Point, along the shoreline where bathing pavilions later stood, although even those are gone now, remembered only by a street named 七姊妹道 meaning seven sisters, which correctly transliterates into English as Tsat Tsz Mui Road. Unlike our own mistranslated Minden, named after a Royal Navy ship to recall the 1759 Battle of Minden, our street's name in Cantonese is Myanmar, formerly Burma. Our club on Minden Row, we have nothing to do with Burma. Even if it is possible to crossover a hump to get here, this isn't the "over the hump" air route of that long vanished airline, the one that ferried legal and not-so-legal cargo to and from Burma during and after the second war.

Our only crime was being bargirls at Seven Sisters.

And girls like us are better off dead, at least while we still answer to "girl" instead of woman, the way I did. The way I still do. I'm not old enough to be forgotten. None of us are. Which is why they all come when I call, these girls who were not privileged to ever become women, no matter how old they were when they died.

Men don't lie to whores. I once had a lover who had been

MI5. He was gentle though, and sometimes cried after he fucked me. The man who killed me was rough and never cried. He kept two fierce Alsatians in his bathtub. That's the trouble with Hong Kong flats, too small for dogs, especially large ones, but some people insist on having them. This man, an English police inspector, he was Vice. Those dogs were hungry the night they ripped me apart and almost tore his left hand off in the process. He still has the scar. The photo in the newspaper caught it when he put up his hand to cover his face the day he was arrested, although that happened years later, long after I was gone. Jail ended his career but he just went to the mercenaries. There's always a place in the world for the rough ones. About my death though, that was an accident. He lost control of his hounds and they savaged my jugular and feasted on my flesh until he muzzled them. Afterwards he hid my corpse because what else could he do? First, though, he cleanly sliced off my hands and feet to be found with no canine teeth marks, separated from the rest of me. It saddens me that the American sailor was wrongly accused. He, the police inspector, pinned it on him. Easy because the other girls saw me go off with sailor boy. They didn't know Alistair came by after he left and took me to his home with the dogs. So that's my story. And now I have no feet to walk or hands to cradle my favorite *fleurs*. All I can do is talk my story till someone hears me.

"Kowloon, Hong Kong" was silly pop, sung in our day, with its choppy chop-chop 2/4 or 4/4 time, like the impossible waltz that is "Chopsticks." We didn't say "TST" back then, since we were mostly Cantonese and said 尖沙嘴, Tsimshatsui; the impossible English of our district's name confounded foreigners who showed up later, in the 1980s and '90s amid rampant nightlife (and day life as well), and our neighborhood was abbreviated to TST, an acronym better suited to a parasitic bloodsucker, the tsetse fly.

We were poorer then, during the four decades before and after the second war, even though wealth lined some of the lanes, avenues, streets and roads of TST. We came to TST because of that wealth and the men who haunted the district, trolling for love, gluttonous with desire. But we were happier then because any money is better than being impoverished. After all, we were young and pretty enough, smart and hungry enough, sad and desperate enough to go away and stay away in TST, far from the shanties or villages or homes of our birth. Those homes where love was absent and our desire for more translated into lust for a future that could be our own. We came in droves during war and peace time, hunting out a perch to land for what passed as a lifetime.

So here I am beginning at the end, or what you out there think of as the end. I am dead, have been dead since the mid-seventies. Alistair scattered my hands and feet in some kind of perverse ritual. My left hand propped by the back entrance to the Peninsula Hotel, the one we sometimes used to enter the kitchen where his friend Gaston the chef served us scrumptiously gourmet dinners for free. It surprises me Gaston did not recognize my hand when he found it. After all, I was sometimes payment for those meals, jacking him off in his office while Alistair waited outside. My left foot he tossed in the harbor, late one night, from the Star Ferry pier in TST. It didn't sink to the depths and landed on a ledge where it wavered precariously, never tipping into the sea. Someone found it and turned it in to the police, and it was preserved as evidence for a while until the case was closed and it eventually rotted away. My right hand and foot were never found.

We girls don't mind though where a story begins. We have, as we like to say, all the time in the world, so sometimes we begin in the middle, other times at the beginning, and often enough at the end. It doesn't much matter how you tell a story, as long as you tell it. This is my story so I'll tell it however I want.

I don't like the beginning of my story. Remembering myself in long pigtails when I really was a girl just makes me miserable. I had a cloth doll Ah-Ma sewed for me and I hung onto her and called her little Miss, the polite form of address for a young lady. *Siu jie!* I'd admonish, *where have you been? Don't you know it's dangerous out there at night you stay with me and I'll take care of you.* It was what Ma used to say before she died, TB or something I'm not sure but I remember she coughed a lot. Pa sold me. I was twelve with buds for breasts and had only just begun menstruating. It was summer. He dragged me out of bed in the middle of the night and hosed me down like one of the pigs. A woman undid my pigtails and combed out my hair. She put me in a thin dress, stuck a pair of sandals with plastic flowers on my feet and took me away from the village. I was too scared to speak or even cry. The last memory I have of Pa is a vision of his back to me, walking away towards our hut. He never even said goodbye.

And then for a while — I'm not sure how long, maybe three or four months — it was a cyclical blur of sleep, food, nights, men, men, men, and more men, until nothing they did could ever hurt again.

Until Monsieur Autre.

That wasn't his name but it was what we girls called him. He was French, but he spoke our language very well, had lived in Taiwan where he said he studied Mandarin and was in Hong Kong teaching French, and he spoke Cantonese too. He visited Auntie Lam, our mamasan, once a week, always asking for her freshest flower. Usually he chose Little Pear or

Night Blossom — they were sixteen and eighteen but dressed to pass for younger — until I arrived at Seven Sisters.

So this is the real beginning of my story, when I became M. Autre's "little cabbage," his special *amour.*

I met him the night of my debut at Seven Sisters. It's a fancy word, debut. Some American sailor taught me that. *It was my sister's debut,* he said, and when I asked him what it meant, he said that where he came from, young girls were presented to society at a ball for debutantes to make their debut. His sister wore a pretty white dress like all her girlfriends and young men escorted the girls so everyone could check her out and see how special she was, and one day one of those young men would make her his bride. The sailor was a gentle man, soft spoken, whose English swayed like a willow in a typhoon. He didn't wear a naval uniform but from the haircut you knew he was one of them. *An officer,* Auntie Lam whispered when she assigned me. *Treat him nice and he'll give you a big tip, maybe even buy you something special.* He kept me a whole weekend. *Did one of them marry your sister,* I wanted to know. *No,* he said, *she died.* He was silent after that and I didn't have the heart to ask what happened. His name was Jefferson, *like the president* was what he said.

But Jefferson was during Vietnam, long after M. Autre, a time when Tsimshatsui was flooded with boys who waddled like ducks. Those were good days, when all us girls made money, when Seven Sisters was busy every night. Even that was a long time ago, and now TST is all about jewelry stores and designer boutiques for mainland tourists or massage parlors where the girls make a pittance for their slavery. The flower markets are gone, along with the food markets and 好好, our favorite won ton noodle haunt. The good days are over and we, despite all our talk, are forever dead.

You see what I mean about our talk-stories? We have

so many middles there are no beginnings. M. Autre though, he looked after me for a time, so I suppose he was a kind of beginning.

The day he finally left, he told me his real name. It was difficult and he laughed when I tried to say Archambault. *So long,* I complained, *why do you people make such long names? Chinese so much easier!* I've always wondered, after he left, why he told me his name. He didn't ask me to remember him like some johns do. Nor did he tell me to look him up if I was ever in Paris the way others occasionally will. As if I would ever go to Manhattan, Kansas, which is where one john was from. He wrote down his address and phone number, insisted I keep the torn slip of paper. I threw it out the minute he left. Such a boy, sweet-faced, told me he wanted to show me off to his friends, to introduce me to his mother. "*Dor yu!* many fish!" as M. Autre would say, making us all laugh at his deliberate mistranslation by mispronouncing the tones for 多 餘, meaning something superfluous or a pointless endeavor. He taught me a lot of English words and phrases, and a little French, although sometimes I think he was poking fun by teaching me deliberately wrong words and phrases. *Don't make me look like a fool,* I'd complain and his answer always was *you could never be a fool.*

Was I a fool? Now that I have all the time in eternity, it is the only question that still vexes and nags. All those sexy clothes and bright shiny things, just to earn a few dollars from so many johns I lost count. Wasn't there anything else I could have done? M. Autre, he often said, why don't you go back to school, learn something, but honestly, that would be *way* too many fishes! He was just as much to blame, don't you think, because he liked fresh girls? And I was young and fresh and even though my hymen was already torn and too many cocks had come before his, he could still pretend I was his baby girl. Pedophile, that's all he was. It doesn't matter now how nicely he treated me, all he wanted was to fuck a child and there's something so vile and wrong-headed about that, so . . . *unnecessary*, this burning desire of his. Don't you think?

You know, I don't even know to whom I'm speaking anymore. Look around, it's always only the girls who come when I call. Many of our johns are just as dead as us but do you see them here? No. Bang, bang, thank you ma'am, as the sailors used to say. And then they get to sleep the sleep of the dead. Meanwhile we're wandering, exhausted, famished ghosts with no hope of rest. What we're looking for to appease our restless spirit we'll never find, and what we need to still our hunger pangs is lost to that heaven where emperors rule and girls must remain girls forever.

Listen to me, it's not too late. You can still fix things. Girls are not pigs to be hosed down and sold. We all return to where Seven Sisters once stood because it's the closest thing to home. But the club's long gone, and even the abandoned space that stayed vacant for so many years has been transformed into a third-rate restaurant, famous mostly for its rat population. Maybe it's just as well it's gone, although for every Seven Sisters that dies, a new one is born elsewhere in TST. You'd think one of those johns would at least come back and visit, maybe look for one of us? Like Manhattan, Kansas and his earnest plea that I should come visit? Oh sure, they've had their wives and daughters or girlfriends and maybe even other younger, fresher girls. But I can't go very far because my feet are gone and I can't reach out to strangle the ones who are still alive because my hands are gone as well. It's a hell of an eternity and if you had any sense you'd do something to turn this world around, find some way to right the wrongs, figure out a better way for me to die.

Listen to me, it's not about fate. We girls love to chatter on about fate because it's a small comfort to think that really, there's nothing to be done so why not just shut up and die the hand you're dealt? But look at us, we're all here, and we haven't shut up, not like those johns whose dead-to-the-world sleep is peacefully silent. If there's one thing I'm sure of is that I have to keep talking-story until you hear me, until you truly listen, until you fix this mess you call life. Fix things so that girls like me can become women, need not always be enslaved, stripped, beaten, fucked, or treated like dolls, created just to satisfy impersonal lusts. You *will* hear us, me, one of these days, because I know you can if you try.

Listen, it's never too late. Just listen.

APPETITES

You can only [fill in the verb] so much before you die.

1. Eat
2. Feast
3. Gorge
4. Drink
5. Imbibe
6. Intoxicate
7. Copulate
8. Lust
9. Lech
10. Couple
11. Uncouple
12. Polygamize
13. Addict
14. Abstain
15. Overdose
16. Breakdown
17. Recover
18. Imbalance
19. Balance
20. Live

But for the Grace

When saw we thee a stranger, and took thee in?
Or naked, and clothed thee?
—Matthew 25:38 (King James)

LET me be blunt: I, too, have courted desperation. It's almost inevitable when we all are just a wee bit mad around the edges, whether or not we're actually bipolar, psychotic, schizophrenic, manic, clinically depressed, ADD, catatonic. Or just plain mad. Our longings are madder, fed by desires that were once unvoiced, unstaged, unknown. The sheep and goats, there's no division now. Three times before the cock crowed, marking the end of my terrible twenties.

By the time I left that terrible time behind, I no longer trusted what I thought I saw, or heard, in those three desperate, desperate pleas.

§

The first time, a student in my co-ed dorm. He was skinny-tall, this pothead with the Einstein hair. We talked occasionally, intimate strangers as we walked across our cold, cold campus, back when climate was not yet changed. By early October, winter edged out autumn and spring thaw could last till mid-May. For sure he had a name, but that has vanished into the cesspool of oblivion. We were all oblivious, hippy-happy, because pot was rampantly sweet. It was the early '70s.

Having jumped ahead a semester in credits, I was a tween, no longer a junior but not yet a senior. It was my second year as RA, resident assistant, a job that offered a room of one's own and half the board. The dining hall was more than the horn of plenty. As a foreign student on the F-1 visa, with employment limited to on-campus work, I needed anything to reduce the cost of what was, for my family, an expensive American college education. Even though it wasn't the Ivies, or New York City, or somewhere comparable to my far more cosmopolitan Hong Kong world even before its economic rise. It was long before Asia dared thumb its nose at the West, the way it can now when the West is no longer the promise of tomorrow. Restraint before globalized desire seduced, enlarging our appetites, before greed, and debt, were good.

So there I was upstate in the far east, due north of New York City, at the smallest four-year SUNY, wandering the corridors of Kent Hall, the dorm with a party reputation because it had previously been all male. Compared to the cat fights I broke up during my previous year at the all-female dorm, my current women's wing was relatively calm, and roommates were not changing as often as underwear. So there I was in Kent, my last year in college, feeling mature enough, at nineteen, to handle the quaintly sexual innuendo of a guy dorm gone gal.

Winter had not yet completely arrived, just as Watergate had not. The unsuitable blond boyfriend had already dumped me and my desperation had moved well past a Dorothy Parker imitation suicide. I even felt slightly superior to my Algonquin heroine, because counseling controlled my emotions sufficiently so that I did not need to try a second time, the way Parker did, also unsuccessfully. We are women, hear us roar, a mere man did not rule our self-worth. Faith in feminism and psychology.

So when a ruckus burst the nighttime silence out in the hallway—I was the RA on duty that evening—I opened my door. A group of guys had forcibly stripped him, that pothead with the Einstein hair, brought him upstairs to the gals' floor, where they dumped him outside my room, right in the middle of the wing. As I opened my door I heard his plea, No, please, not my underpants. His captors had raced off as several other doors opened to peer at his cowering nakedness. He met my eyes, Cover me please. I grabbed a blanket, threw it over him, shoved him into my room and closed the door. Called his RA, said, Bring clothes. An incident over almost as quickly as it had begun.

But for years I could not un-see, could not un-hear his anguished face, his whimpering plea. A quarter of a century later, I tried to articulate it as fiction in a workshop in San Francisco, and failed. Columbine had not yet happened then and *Mean Girls* was still six years in the future.

Meanwhile, back in the past, life carried on as if nothing had changed. But he no longer met my eyes when we ran into each other. He wanted to avoid me, and we never spoke again after that night.

Spring eventually arrived.

The sky was clear the day he was arrested. This was a more distant ruckus, across campus at the science building, one I rarely entered. As the grapevine buzzed, I thought of him—quiet but intelligent, less the pothead he appeared to be, more the smart but awkward kid who didn't fit in. We had talked a little music and philosophy back when we still spoke. Eventually the facts emerged: He had assembled a bomb to blow up the chemistry lab. How long had he hunted down that information in the library? How slowly and patiently had he found what he needed, at the local hardware store undoubtedly, or perhaps even in the labs at college? Patty Hearst was recently a headline. If you can't lick 'em, join 'em, could that have been his credo? Terrorism begins at home before it explodes on the rest of society.

And the more things change, the more they don't. "Clothe the Naked" is a short story by Dorothy Parker from the 1930s, about a blind black boy who goes forth proudly one day in his new hand-me-down suit his single mother obtains from her rich employers. The laughter and derision he encounters in the street sends him fleeing back home, cowed. There is no redemption.

§

The second time, a colleague at the airline in Hong Kong. The unsuitable first Scottish husband was already divorced and I had abandoned the rebound Chinese fiancé. The roar of my womanhood equaled "choosing" the men I slept with and dumped, the sting of that first rejection by the blond in college never completely un-stung. It was difficult to recognize my immaturity, though, when hormones and insecurities abounded. *Sex and the City* was still a future non-shock, and *Fear of Flying* the moment's benchmark.

If part of a bee stinger remains unremoved, the body will eventually swallow it up somehow, although the online jury chatter is still out on that score. The medical community says to remove the stinger as soon as possible. However, even they concede that the oft-stung individual can build immunity. Not unlike the sex act, because promiscuity simply inoculates one against heartbreak, or so my terrible twenties were bent on proving. In my books, Erica Jong was a scaredy-pussycat.

Is sex something we actually need if procreation is not the point?

He was Audit, I was Advertising. It was my second to the last year in the job because the call of the wild was growing louder, seducing me away from my promiscuous but boring business world in favor of the writer-in-progress. As an odd Asian female who traveled frequently for work in the region (but was not a flight attendant), I was once again a tween, neither properly female and certainly not male. Company regulations meant I always wore skirts and heels. There was no mistaking my gender although my survival depended on being one of the boys.

It was also a colonial era, when white boys ruled, although the local Chinese boys were beginning to rise, at least in Hong Kong. Nixon had already been to China and it was just before Carter tore down the bamboo curtain. Hong Kong's international airline was a capitalist, for-profit British 行 (or Hong), unlike the nationalized carriers in most Asian nations. Airlines were monopolies. Flying wasn't cheap and the industry still profitable, although that reality was already sliding down slipperier and slipperier slopes of consumer demand. My pay was good, the benefits brilliant, and the Western men roving and roaring around the region succumbed greedily to yellow fever. Few Asian women roared, which meant that those of us who did had our pick of men. As long as love and marriage were off the table, since the majority of rovers were about to be, or were otherwise engaged to one of their own. A tight Asian pussy, I was actually told by more than one Western lover, was my great asset. "Lover" was a kinder, gentler name; many were merely sex partners. It was easy to be heartless in such a world.

Onto my plane hopped the kinder, gentler audit man. He was a local Chinese, a few years older than me, reporting, as I did, to a white man boss. It was only in Operations among the flight attendants and ground staff, or at Customer Service, that Chinese (including some women) were promoted to management. On the business side, Sales had Chinese managers, but all the other departments were headed by British executives, or the odd Australian like my boss. The revolution was still a tea party, which would have made Chairman Mao turn in his grave.

Let me be blunt: He was a hopeless lover. A virgin, clunky, stuck in the local culture that shaped him, having busted ass to get to where he was. With my foreign university degree,

English language, and Western cultural fluency, I was more tween than he ever could hope to be, able to hang with the white world as readily as the local one, the way the Chinese university grads on the executive track could, even though I was not one of them. What was the attraction? That he took my position seriously? That he talked to me as an equal? That he would never outrank me, the way I knew the other Chinese executives all would in time, because a woman, even one on the executive track, would never rise as quickly? I knew my pay outstripped his, even though I was a far more recent hire. Life divided us, sexual experience divided us, education divided us, language divided us, class divided us. I lived in my own place, he did not, as most locals lived at home. He had a girlfriend, a good girl, a virgin, for whom he was saving money to marry. I was just the whore.

Except that I wasn't, not really. We became sort-of friends. I took him to the restaurants and places in my privileged Hong Kong world which he did not know how to access. I paid my own way, something that rarely happened on dates back then. And afterwards, even though it became less and less something that felt right to do, I brought him to my bed.

On our last date—I forget where we ate, but it was likely something in my repertoire—he said, teach me please. Show me how to live in your world and let me be a part of it. I can learn. Take me please.

His gaze unnerved me. My immorality flooded me and I felt deeply ashamed. What right did I have to lead him on, to let this friendship move beyond the platonic? I could just have been a decent friend. My sexual dance card was already over-full. What perverse greed was this, what perverse gluttony for more and more men to notch on my bedpost?

I cannot unsee his shocked humiliation when I said no, I can't, and then told him we should no longer see each other. He accepted it, though, civilly enough. It was not the heartbreak of love I cursed him with, but the heartbreak of his lot in life, having been "allowed" to glimpse something more.

I cannot unsee this former geek lover, with his open mind, decent command of English, and curiosity that allowed him to see the world beyond his borders.

It is too easy, in this era, to point out that he was not offering me love, just himself as an apprentice to my privileged upbringing so that he could return to his girlfriend with the benefit of his romantic education. It is easy to claim a no-fault separation, and reject the guilty conscience. When I finally left the company, and Hong Kong, he asked if he could have the MOMA-imitation plastic chairs and coffee table in my flat, which I gave him. They were off-white and compact, suited to the tiny spaces of our city. By then he was engaged. It was the closest he could come to slapping me in the face.

Why pin the blame on myself, an immature donkey girl?

But to pretend blamelessness is to live the unexamined life. I was wrong, wrong, wrong. When you hold all the cards you do not, no, should not seduce into your game one who is bound to lose. We say, as women, that we need a level playing field. Yet when I could have leveled it, I did not. Morality is more than just for public display. It matters in our private lives, perhaps even more, because no one might ever see or hear or know.

Yet it is that un-removable bee stinger that troubles me most. What I know now but wish I knew then is that for many years after this moment, I would still engage in conflicted affairs of the body and heart. I have never been a fan of *Sex and the City*. It strikes me as hypocritical, a pretense to leveling the playing field when, in fact, the real desire is to perpetuate happily ever after marital bliss. It would be many more years before I could define an honorable way to couple, before I could leave behind the desire to show off my "superior" womanhood. Power corrupts, regardless of gender. Just as shucking off the past and never taking responsibility is the no-fault slippery slope which may, if we are not careful, collapse all semblance of our civilized world. Today, Kristen Roupenian's "Cat Person." What worse dystopia tomorrow?

§

The third time, a female professional acquaintance who wanted to be more of a friend. She could tan dark, like me, and we both readily eschewed the pure ideal of white Chinese skin, content with our natural pigmentation. She was also from Hong Kong and traveled as much as I did, possibly more, even to places that then seemed exotic to us: Bahrain and Dubai. Her career path had been tougher than mine, harder scrabbled, far less privileged. We met sometime during the last few months at my airline job, by which time I had already decided to quit and disappear to Greece to write. Already I was transitioning— the book of the day was Gail Sheehy's *Passages*, which I never read but probably should have—jogging from the straight and narrow to the crooked and jagged path. What I didn't know then but wish now I did was that I would have to tread all four paths, and many, many more, because a single fork in the path was already dead-white imagery.

Her name I have forgotten, but shouldn't have. What I do remember are her wild, curly locks, almost a soft 'fro—I wondered if foreign blood had flowed into the river of her Chinese heritage—and strikingly large eyes. She had a beak-like mouth, thin lips, and small, even, very white teeth. Let me bluntly stereotype: The "average" Hong Kong Chinese man would have given her wide berth, but the "average" white man on our waterfronts would have trailed after her, salivating.

It is possible she and I met on board a flight, but memory is the crookedest path, and most historical facts are irrelevant in the long run. We became acquainted, that is a fact, because we were both in marketing, even though I was trying to remove its malingering hold on me in favor of "art." I had the grandeur of ideals! To write, to live free, to be an unfettered woman, to escape the bourgeoisie of my birth, to abandon the Chinese world of my origins in favor of an international literary self. Marguerite Duras and Doris Lessing wrote my guidebooks, and *The Second Sex* was still not yet past a use-by date. The problem of being twenty-something is that you believe you need never grow old. I had a better handle on mortality at eleven-plus, when I used to imagine the death of my parents, as well as my own eventual demise.

Our acquaintance was short. I remember little of what we did together except for one conversation. Where we were or what surrounded us has vanished into some twilight zone. What remains are her smile, her bared teeth, her dark complexion and beautifully coiffed black hair, her sharp red outfit with its fitting skirt, her high heels, her throaty laugh, her voice lowered as she said I love to travel and talk to men, especially Western ones, don't you? And then, without missing a beat, They're so much better for sex. It was a perfect T-Zone moment, when the protagonist finally realizes the inescapable horror of her situation. I did not respond, but she kept at me, wanting to share what she likely considered the similar shape of our lives.

In our contemporary shorthand, I "ghosted," "unfriended," "blocked" her. Resisted this ebony bird beguiling, afraid to confront the truth of my existence. As this was even before voicemail, I took most of my social calls at work, where a receptionist or secretary took her messages that I never returned. Eventually, her calls stopped. I cannot unsee her absence or my own mean-girl spirit. What's good for the goose only applies to one goose, alone on her hill. Mommie

Dearest loves you, or at least, until she doesn't, which is when, as the young screen version of Christina Crawford says, "she can make you disappear." Had I heeded Poe's raven in this instance, I might have trod an easier path in my endlessly examined life.

§

In later years, well after my terrible twenties during which these three sightings occurred, I would encounter many other naked strangers. I would continue to make the mistake of believing that there, but for the grace of some spiritual force, was the face of my own fate. It is only now, in connecting what I cannot unsee to what I should not have unseen, that the meaning of this oft-used phrase comes at me in full bloom. It is a pretentiously kind notion, a shudder of existential horror at this—a victim of bullying, war, school shooting, bombing, terrorist act; a homeless panhandler; the blind, maimed, deformed, insane, or otherwise "othered" human being; the collaterally damaged. It is easy to shudder at such strangers, followed by looking away. It is only now, in re-looking, re-seeing, even re-hearing, that a re-envisioning occurs. I could have been less neurotic and still lived an examined life. But don't ask now to replace what could've and should've with what has been, is, and will always be.

Instead, allow me to re-see in exchange for just a little grace.

Two

Monkey in Residence

IN the spring of 2017, just after the grave sweeping 清明 festival, the Government of the Hong Kong SAR[8] proudly announced funding for a new Academic Chair position — Monkey in Residence — to be given to the public universities. Its objective was to honor our famous ancestor, that half god, half mortal Monkey[9]. Monkey, as everyone knew, had sired several heirs and the dynasties of Monkeys that followed were, the government claimed, *a significant family of special Chinese citizens from whom we should learn more about our own history, travels and culture. What better place than at those institutes of higher learning where young minds are molded and refined?*

All over the city, huge posters with the character "Monkey"[10] appeared, announcing a "logo design and naming contest" for the new Chair position. The electronic poster was also all over the Internet and even had its own Facebook page.

猴

Money in Resident
Logo Dissent & Numbing Concert for new Char
Prize $11,980.20

---

8 **SAR** Special Administrative Region of the People's Republic of China, a.k.a. Hong Kong's postcolonial neocolonial status under its then sovereign ruler.

9 **Monkey** is Sun Wukong, more commonly known as the Monkey King, a mythological figure who travels with the Buddhist monk Xuanzang to the western regions of China through Central Asia and India to obtain the sacred Buddhist texts or sutras. Monkey's story is told in the 16th Century Chinese novel *Journey to the West* 西遊記 (Xiyou Zi in pinyin). The novel is considered one of the four great classical novels of Chinse literature, and is generally attributed to 吳承恩 Wu Chengen. Monkey's descendants in Hong Kong are a speculative family but judging by the growing population of monkeys in evidence throughout the city, this speculation may be less fictional than it appears.

10 **Monkey:** 猴 (hou), Mandarin, although in Hong Kong the Cantonese equivalent 馬騮 (maa lau) was what locals used.

It took about a week, but the posters were eventually replaced with all "typos" fixed and the prize money corrected to $12,000[11]. A government spokeswoman blamed the errors on their communications department intern from one of the universities' English department, whose recently appointed Acting Head was heard to declare *my English is not very good, ha! ha! ha!* At least he was correct about that, his colleagues whispered, beleaguered as they were by the third Acting Head to be installed in less than two years. The government spokeswoman was however quick to add *this error is inconsequential as the Chinese language version is correct, and, after all, most in Hong Kong know Chinese, ha! ha! ha!* Laughter by the powers-that-be had recently become a trend, a fashionable way to soften bad or fake news. Most of us nodded in agreement, although a few running dogs dissented, those long-resident leftover colonial British or BBCs[12] who neither read nor spoke Chinese. We wondered when these latter would get fed up and leave, sooner rather than later some wished, although others said why care as long as they fed our economy, *and anyway,* we whispered, *English and Chinese* (Mandarin and Cantonese) *are both our official languages, so we can be bi- or even tri-lingual, right?* Far more complaints were heard about the prize money. Where was the missing $19.80? Was this corruption or a mistake? Inquiring minds wanted to know on Weibo, Instagram, even on LinkedIn. Certainly along our vines the whispers spread across the city. Eventually, the government's Financial Secretary (FS) gave in after much pressure by the Dean of Business at HKU, the leading university. The FS was a graduate of HKU, but, as everyone

11 **Hong Kong dollars** in 2019 were pegged to the US dollar at the rate of approximately 7.8 to 1 USD, meaning the prize was worth a little over US$1,500, which strikes us as a paltry sum for some human to design a logo and provide a name for what was an extremely expensive salaried position for a Monkey (or human, for that matter).

12 **BBC:** British born Chinese or the British Broadcasting Corporation. The difference is academic.

knew, his myopic focus on the bottom line greatly surpassed his common sense.

Meanwhile, the excitement among Monkey's descendants was palpable.

"What are my chances do you think?" Monkey Fire Hero III asked. At age ten, he was eldest son of his generation and leader of the fire clan in Hong Kong. The grandeur and power of a Chair Professorship gleamed in his mind, although he was loath to admit it.

His inner circle of younger male fire clan Monkeys were quick to say he definitely *must* be the choice. After all, who else was more brilliant, more virile, more important than he? Flattery, they knew, would keep him calm. His violent temper erupted whenever his face was lost, which happened often, given his propensity for pompous declarations about his power and achievements. They quickly diverted his attention by nonstop chattering.

"How do you think they'll make the decision?"

"Is it one at each, or just one position that all universities compete for?"

"You don't suppose they'll consider," this, followed by a wince, "*female* Monkeys, do you?"

"D'you think he has to be a graduate from one of the universities? Or if not, one who graduated with honors from a top international one?"

All the others tried to shush this last speaker. A young son-in-law who had newly entered the inner circle, he was unaware of Monkey Fire Hero III's sensitivity about his abysmal academic record. As recently as last year, their leader had gone to great lengths, *again,* to try to have his grades altered or redacted and to have an honorary PhD conferred on him by either Oxford or Harvard. Unsuccessfully, as it turned out, because there was no one left to bribe or do his bidding.

Really, at his age, they all whispered, wondering why it should matter anymore? Luckily, their great leader appeared not to have heard, his short attention span interrupting, as always.

But their clan's Chief Financial Officer Dickson, a non-Monkey human, declared. "This is a ridiculous idea."

Dickson rarely spoke. When he did, the fire Monkeys listened. There was a long-ish silence, punctuated by teeth picking, spitting and banana peeling. When in doubt, fire Monkeys were given to the long pause. Finally, Fire Hero III himself spoke up. "Why should that be ridiculous?"

"Think about it," Dickson said. "How many Monkeys go to our universities in Hong Kong? Zero. Okay, maybe a few of the cross-bred Monkey-Humans do, but they're mostly females so they don't count, because females can get away with treason. Most of the male cross-breeds hang out in the trees with you all. This government is just trying to placate you, to make you feel important so that you'll vote them back in at the next election. It's all about politics, all about the restlessness among the Intelligent Beasts. Who among the beasts caused the most havoc at the last election? The Monkeys, of course, since . . ." and here he glanced sideways at the others, "the smart humans know that Monkeys, especially Fire Monkeys, are by far the most intelligent. So this is one of the FS's famous "sweeteners" — toss them a bonus and they'll be content."

He took a breath, sucked on his inhaler, and continued. "Even you, honorable leader, attended the University for Intelligent Beasts on the Chinese exclave island territory, Feiyudao[13]. That's the natural order of things, where Monkeys stick with their own kind and return to the trees."

The effort of speaking clearly exhausted him and he

---

13 Feiyudao (飛魚島) or Flying Fish Island is a speculative geographical location in the mode of Jonathan Swift's floating island Laputa, as depicted in the third book of *Gulliver's Travels*. Likewise, the University of Intelligent Beasts bears some resemblance to the Academy on Laputa.

slumped back in his chair to continue gazing at the spreadsheets on his screen.

The long pause was interrupted, too soon, by the same young son-in-law. "Feiyudao? Do you mean Tobiuo-Shima?"

Once again, a noisy shushing followed. Didn't this kid know *anything?* Just because he had majored in Japanese — a serious mistake, many in the clan believed, for their leader's youngest daughter by his tenth concubine to have married this cultural traitor — he still was Chinese and should have known better than to refer to Pinnacle Point Island of the contested Diaoyus by its Japanese name! Especially within earshot of his father-in-law.

Finally Fire Monkey III spoke. "Thank you Dickson. We will take your concern under advisement."

Ω

Meanwhile, at the University Institute of the City of Kowloon, or U-ICK for short, Jasper Man-ming Mui, the now-former intern at the communications department of the Government of Hong Kong, was basking in subversive glory. In his dorm room at U-ICK, school mates surrounded him, notably two popular girls, Punny Li and Anita Chan, who had previously paid him scant attention.

"What made you do it?" they all wanted to know.

"I was inspired. It's like Professor Kendrick says, language is the tool of the user. Master the tool and you have power. On his walls hung the framed "erroneous" poster. He had ensured a large stash did not get destroyed and already, a frenzied international bidding war had begun for this latest collectible. The electronic version still existed in cyberspace, protected by a firewall so thick not even the hackers in North Korea could crack it.

Jasper was seated next to YK Tseng, his best friend and

hacker extraordinaire, who already had a scholarship for grad school at MIT to where he was headed in September.

"What are you going to do now, Jasper?" YK asked.

It was no secret he could be placed on academic probation, maybe even expelled, and if so no other government university would likely offer him a place. His only recourse would be one of the private colleges. Unlike YK, he did not see his future at a university abroad. He shrugged, nonchalant. "No idea. Maybe I'll start a new bilingual news magazine and report on the corruption in government."

Punny, who majored in Veterinary Science, spoke up. "You two should start a new political party. All the democracy and independence parties have collapsed. Give people hope. This government resorts to such low tactics. Bribing Monkeys, imagine!"

Jasper beamed. He had been crushing on Punny all year but she barely knew he existed, until now. This was worth it. Who cared if U-ICK threw him out? There was more to life than a university degree. Of course, his parents thought otherwise but for the moment, he silenced his mind of their disapproval, and instead pictured Punny, her skintight jeans and panties around her ankles as he humped her.

Not to be outdone, Anita, who like Jasper, was an English major, said. "The news magazine is a much better idea. After all, language is your talent, not politics." Punny shot her an angry look. Undaunted, she continued. "I'd help you with that and so would my friends at HKU." Her reference to the city's top university was deliberate. She knew it would flatter Jasper whose English ability surpassed most local students. His overall grades just hadn't been good enough to get him into HKU, and he had had to settle for U-ICK instead.

"We'll see," Jasper said. "Professor Wan has already 'sumoned' me to a meeting." He pulled up the email from the Acting Head of English. "Look, he has five spelling or grammar errors in two short sentences. Fuck his mother, why should I care what he thinks? He's a joke."

Everyone agreed, although Punny remained silent. Wan was a professor at Vet Science where she badly wanted a lucrative research post. He had promised to support her, so she didn't dare bad mouth him, even though she knew it was only because he wanted to get into her pants.

But Anita spoke up, since the rumors around Wan had trailed him into English. "What's the matter Punny, don't you agree? Or is Wan too, aah… salty-wet-horny around you?"

Punny blushed and fled the room. Jasper, who hadn't known this bit of gossip, felt his heart balloon pop. But, having slain her rival, Anita had already sidled up next to him in her micro skirt and filmy, skimpy top, a willing substitute for his gaze.

A noisy and confused debate ensued until YK declared he was hungry, and the group headed out to the nearby hawker stands at the wet market for late night soup noodles and congee.

Ω

By September, Fire Monkey III was installed as the first Professor Monkey in Residence in the city. No one was really surprised at this choice — what other Monkey could the government possibly have picked? — although what did surprise us was that U-ICK was the first university granted this honor. What an insult to HKU! After all, it had been in existence since 1911, and was a *proper* university, while U-ICK was a former Polytech that only gained university stature in 1984. *Furthermore*, the whispers along our vines breathed, *HKU has ivy-covered walls while U-ICK is mostly bare concrete, except for us morning glories*. It was a tut-tutting moment in academia. Even Fire Monkey III briefly pondered this curious situation, but being a monkey, he quickly moved on to more important matters. And his number one concern was the greening of U-ICK.

"Trees," he declared at his Distinguished Chair lecture, "this campus needs more trees and vines. It will improve the learning environment if students learn to live in nature. We must plant a rain forest on the roof of the rotunda at the top of the hill. That will be perfect."

The Financial Secretary, who was in the audience, leapt up to applaud Professor Monkey in Residence; trees were cheaper than buildings or labs and *anyone* could plant trees! All the faculty and most of the students also rose. The President, who had dozed off, staggered to his feet. He did not want a Professor Monkey in Residence, but the FS had forced this position on his university. President Ma was afraid Monkey would foment revolt among the hundreds of emotional support animals registered at the university in recent years. Already, the campus resembled a giant petting zoo, what with the chihuahuas, Pomeranians, shih tzus, Siamese and Persian cats, geckos, cockatoos, parakeets, even kingfishers and cormorants, peacocks, plus the odd snake or two hanging out with their student companions. He had wanted to draw a line at snakes, given the poisonous species in the territory, but SPAS, the Society for the Prevention of Alienation of Snakes had protested for twenty-five days, forcing him to cancel his vacation, until he succumbed.

President Ma's distress increased as applause thundered through the auditorium. How he wished he had never established his Institute of Cross-Border Veterinary Science & Technology. ICE-VEST, as it was known, had become his albatross. He had not expected the alarming demand for emotional support animals by the students, something most faculty supported. Their revenge. He had diverted salary monies out of other academic departments into ICE-VEST, and no one could replace retired or departed faculty. His hope was to tap into scientific research funds from China — swine or avian flu, hoof and mouth disease, mad cow, were these not worthy of study? Instead, he was mired in an animal farm, and soon a rooftop rainforest that would turn into a planet for apes!

"President Ma?" His assistant's gentle voice nudged him out of his daytime nightmare. Everyone else was seated, while he still stood, applauding weakly, lost in confusion. The mammalian ocean behind him snickered. The President sat down, defeated.

Ω

A week after Monkey's lecture, Jasper attended his hearing by the Academic Disciplinary Council. Professor Cyrus Wan, Acting Head of English presided. The night before Wan had called President Ma, begging him to preside. "You owe me," he said. "I agreed to be Acting Head to force out as many professors as possible to get you more funds for ICE-VEST. I've already done that in three other departments as Acting Head. At *your* request. You can't throw me to the cockroaches now!"

"One last time," Ma said. "I promise no more."

"The media will be there. You know it. The *English language* media! How am I supposed to talk to them? I'll be a laughing stock."

"Don't worry Wan. Just expel the little fuckhead for disrespecting our government, make a one-sentence statement, and leave. Any other questions, just say no comment. You can do it."

Now, Wan was confronted by the student and Professor Kendrick of Linguistics. The proceedings were all in English, since Kendrick was British and all public universities were supposedly "English medium." He tried to focus on the case Jasper was making in his own defense. Kendrick chimed in about the "creative use of language" which the government had simply failed to appreciate. The other professors on the council nodded sagely, made noises about not stifling critical discourse. Wan could see the writing on the wall; they were not willing to punish this student.

Afterwards, outdoors on the grand concourse, Kendrick made statements to the press about freedom of speech and how no crime had been committed. Jasper was allowed to continue his studies and he and Anita produced their bilingual newsletter, much to the dismay of Ma and Wan. The first editorial offered great support to the proposal by Professor Monkey in Residence for the rooftop urban rain forest. Within nine months, the campus had become a jungle and Jasper and Anita staged a naked, communal lie-in beside the lily pond, where the fences were twined by vines of morning glories. Punny did not participate.

Ω

This all happened a long time ago, when Hong Kong still had several universities, before the city erupted in protests led by the Intelligent Beasts. It was a time when we knew change was in the air. After 2047, we no longer were a Special Administrative Region of China, governed by the Basic Law of "one country two systems." The first Monkey in Residence led to others, including several females, and in time, humans learned to swing on vines and ate the bananas, ferns, and morning glories that grew abundantly in our sub-tropical jungle. The buses and subways and cars disappeared, as did the airport and planes, because some humans also learned to fly with the migrating birds and butterflies, while others joined the underground world of rats and snakes.

The universities whittled down to one, U-ICK, because most Hong Kong students flocked to the University for Intelligent Beasts. In 2022, after the roof of the rain forest rotunda collapsed, President Ma tried to flee campus in the wake of the scandal, only to trip over an emotional support boa constrictor whose companion student was out to lunch. The boa, agitated, encircled Ma and strangled him to death. Ma never witnessed the longevity of his ICE-VEST, eventually renamed the Academy for Monkeys in Residence or AM-Res. The renaming was essential, as Jasper and Anita noted in their bilingual online media, *Borderless Hong Kong*, because "cross-border" no longer held any meaning as humans and Intelligent Beasts were rapidly transforming into Humane Intelligent Beasts or HIBs through cross-breeding. When Monkey Fire Hero III finally passed away, at the ripe old age of 45, the whispering along our vines was that *perhaps he really was a baboon because everyone knows monkeys just don't live that long*. But it didn't stop the territory that had been Hong Kong from honoring him with the equivalent of a state funeral. After all, we wouldn't be the wonderful world we are now, if not for that first rooftop rain forest he planted. Despite the roof collapsing, weighted down by undrained water underneath, it accelerated the transformation of our city as nature claimed it back. Besides, he was the first Professor Monkey in Residence. For us, the vines of morning glories, we mostly want to tell the stories of the real heroes, even if they were just history's accidents.

Ω Ω Ω

Morning Glories, Mai Po Marshes, Hong Kong 2019 © Xu Xi

A Brief History of Deficit, Disquiet & Disbelief
by 飛蚊 FeiMan

www.j-dd&d/mydao.net as published in the
academic journal *World Tongue Findings in
English*, Vol 3, Issue 1, 2020, University of Laputa,
PartsUnknown, www.wtf.edu.lap

Note: The Cantonese romanization of the author's name looks deceptively English but is pronounced FAY-MUN, to rhyme with bun, and is likely a pen name. It literally means "Flying Mosquito(es)," Hong Kong Cantonese slang for floaters, those annoying images that flit across your vision, unstoppably, as your eyes age. The writer remains unknown. This found manuscript was on a park bench at Aberdeen Street, Hong Kong, on June 3, 2018.[14] It was evening, so I left the envelope there overnight, thinking the writer would come back and collect it when he or she or they realized its loss. But there it was the next morning, so I took it to publish it, hoping the writer would eventually claim the payment and rights. Since its publication five years earlier, no one has come forward. However it's fair to conclude that the writer is a Hong Kong native, as a mainland Chinese would have used simplifed characters 飞蚊子 (Fei Wenzi) and added the dimunitive 子 at the end as the nomenclature for mosquito. However, the writer might not be Chinese at all since the text is in English, and could be a Taiwanese or Singaporean, or even a white American masquerading as Asian as one poet did, thus resulting in the inclusion of his poem in *Best American Poetry*, Simon & Schuster, 2015.[15]

2018 was the year that the journal *Deficit, Disquiet & Disbelief* (hereinafter "DD&D") ceased operations for good, probably because China had become rather too difficult to ignore about Diaoyu. But for the editors (hereinafter "Anox+1"), this duo would forever after think of their journal's

---

14 Coincidentally, the date *The Journal of Speculative Nonfiction* was announced as a new publication, and submissions solicited by editors Robin Hemley & Leila Philip, where this piece now re-appears in the past, time being mutable in our world.
15 You cannot make this stuff up so you might as well default to fact, and suspend disbelief.

home base as Senkaku, because origins being what they are, mere nomenclature will never transform anyone's worldview.

But my task is to write a brief history of the journal, rather than speculate on the reason for its demise. As a contributor to DD&D[16] the quarterly (the exception was 2006 when one editor came down with typhoid, of all diseases, and they only published two issues of Vol 4), I know enough about its origins and evolution to do so. Besides, I myself am from Feiyudao (Chinese)[17] or Tobiuo-Shima (Japanese),[18] aka Pinnacle Point Island of Diaoyu or Senkaku and so am a native daughter of these islands. There is some dispute as to whether or not my home island really belongs as some argue it is actually an exclave. However that argument is specious, as most thinking persons understand that a floating island will, by its very nature, hover around the borders of the archipelago below, and occasionally will even float beyond those invisible boundaries out to the ocean. It's rather like a child riding her rubber alligator in a swimming pool; you don't expect her to stay in one place. To insist on pinpointing exact coordinates is as pointless as expecting the shouting of opposing facts to cease by those nations claiming ownership of these islands.

However, here are other indisputable facts. Most historians agree that the manuscript "A Short Voyage to the Outer Limits of Japan"[19] by Lemuel Gulliver, unearthed

16 See Vol 11, No 4 ; Vol 9, No 2 ; Vol 7, No 3.
17 飛魚島, literally, the Flying Fish Island as it is indeed somewhat fish-shaped. Pomfret, not swordfish.
18 トビウオ島
19 It has never been determined why our British ancestor left his manuscript behind. This unpublished book of the account of his travels would have helped readers better understand his third book about the voyage to the floating island of Laputa, Feiyudao's sister territory, although we came into existence earlier. The reason I use its Chinese rather than Japanese name is due to my lack of fluency in Japanese, even though I am of partial Japanese ancestry and have hardly any Chinese blood. But China has taken such a hold of all us Feiyudaoists, that we cannot help acquiring at least a nodding acquaintance with their language, while Japan, alas, being the exonym that it is, has lesser claim in the 21st century as a land where the sun originates. This saddens me because I love traveling to Japan, probably even more than traveling

from the caves at the easternmost tip of Feiyudao in 1746 by Chinese speleologists, offers sufficient evidence for our uniquely mongrel origins. Despite his short voyage, Lemuel impregnated a number of Japanese and mixed-race women; these "discomfort women" were forced on him by the Emperor and he was ordered to have sexual relations with them in lieu of his having to trample upon a crucifix, which he declined to do.[20] The women and he were shackled and sent to Tobiuo-Shima as it was then known and which was mostly uninhabited, and trapped there until proof of their loss of virginity was provided to armed soldiers who accompanied them. It is a disturbing history, and the manuscript records Lemuel's helplessness and distaste at having what he termed "unclean intercourse with these strange and terrified foreign girls," because they were mostly "young girls, some barely past puberty, the oldest being no more than twenty years of age." The most shocking aspect of his experience was that these girls had all been *willingly* sacrificed by those wishing to please the Emperor, young virgins offered by families who were shunned because of the unclean intercourse of one of their own, Japanese women who had either been raped by Dutch or Chinese traders, or were prostitues, and who had given birth to mixed-race children. Other families with members who were known to be Christian also sacrificed their girls. In

around China. My acquaintance with English is similar, as Britain, and subsequently the United States, have made such economic and linguistic conquests of our world that even Feiyudaoists all begin studying English at the ridiculously early age of two. What has spurred us onwards to master English has been none other than Mr. Ma himself, the former English teacher and founder of Alibaba who now owns the *South China Morning Post*, Hong Kong's leading English newspaper, a testament to English becoming so global it is virtually Chinese. Yet I am no more British than I am Chinese, although I obviously have English ancestry, but should really be conversant in Dutch, since even Lemuel G (as we refer to our ancestral Big Daddy) pretended to be Dutch when he visited Japan and was conversant in the language.

20 In Book III of *Gulliver's Travels,* the author wrote "fake news" on this point, evading any clear explanation of why the Emperor did not insist he trample a crucifix as other visitors had to during Japan's 200-year isolationist, anti-Christian phase at that time, when only Chinese and Dutch nationals were permitted entry.

other words, the mongrel caste. This was, to him, even more shocking than the further assaults he witnessed by soldiers on these girls during their imprisonment, because "some of these young women developed affection for their captors who rewarded them with extra food or other comforts." It is a fact that several of the soldiers returned to the island later and took up residence alongside the women and their offspring who were not allowed to leave. Lemuel stated that he never wanted to return to this island — the horror was too profoundly distressing a memory— and took no interest thereafter in the numerous progeny that resulted from his "journey of deficit, disquiet, and disbelief." This is of course how DD&D got its name. It may also be the reason why he chose not to publish that book of his travels, and left it behind in the cave that was his dwelling during his month-long stay. However, I digress and speculate as I really should *not* do in the writing of a history, especially given the editor's instructions that I "stick to the facts for a change, *if* you can." (*Note to self:* I don't care for this editor's sarcasm and may cease writing for him soon)

Yet this awful history does not appear particularly unusual when we regard the history of our world, does it?

DD&D was conceived as a travel journal that sought to publish pieces about cosmopolitan life in contemporary Asia "without the least Assistance from Genius or Study."[21] A *little* study might perhaps have made for a more successful launch issue. The by-now infamous line of the editorial manifesto in Vol 1, No 1 to "extoll the beauty and wonder of Senkaku with travel writing that will attract numerous tourists to its shores, especially from China" created, naturally, a controversial clang.

---

21 The editorial manifesto cites this from *Gulliver's Travels* Part III, Ch V "A Voyage to Laputa, Balnibarbi, Glubbdubdrib, Luggnagg, and Japan," echoing the mission of the Advancers of Speculative Learning at the Academy on Laputa, where their famous invention sought to create, among other things, "an universal Language to be understood in all civilized Nations," something the typhoid stricken member of Anox+1 greatly desired DD&D to achieve.

What were Anox+1 thinking ? The year was 2003 and to call the islands "Senkaku" guaranteed the Chinese would take umbrage, which they did. In fact, there are those who believe that the launch issue of DD&D contributed to escalating the political dispute. I should note here that neither one of Anox+1 were Japanese (I say "were" because both editors died shortly after announcing the cessation of publication in what was possibly a seppuku suicide-murder. Anox+1 owned a collection of Samurai artifacts and a bloodied sword was at the scene next to their bowels. But such speculations are better left to the Hong Kong Police who found their bodies on Fei Zyu Dou[22] — the floating island that hovers regularly[23] over Lantau where Hong Kong's international airport is located, much to the distress of Air Traffic Control — that much is fact, their deaths I mean).

Despite its inauspicious beginnings, the journal continued to have a highly successful run for the next few years, attracting thousands of subscribers with their giveaway of a catty[24] of flying fish. They also paid their writers well, in any freely convertible currency of their choice. However, for one piece

22 肥豬島, transliteration Cantonese, literally fat pig island, although locally often referred to as Siu Yuk Dou 燒肉島, meaning roast meat (or pig) island as a fat piglet is ideal for roasting to make this dish.

23 Fei Zyu Dou only came into existence in 1998, the year after Hong Kong's handover to China, at the peak of the Asian Financial Crisis. Its origins are murky, as several journalists then reported that this was undoubtedly the initiative of a cabal of the city's richest property owners and developers, all seeking an offshore haven for their wealth. However, this remains unproven and was decried as "fake news" by the city's second Chief Executive of China's post-colonial rule, the man eventually imprisoned for graft and financial malfeasance, proving yet again that you can only make up some of the facts some of the time before they catch up to you. What is fact is that there are no offshore banks on Fei Zyu Dou, although it is where Columbarium City is located, a development by Flying Wax Death Ltd. www.flyingwaxdeath.net; this Hong Kong Stock Exchange listed company has made huge profits selling expensive columbariums to the city's population desperate to secure afterlife property for their loved ones in Hong Kong's over-priced real estate market, even for the dead. How the company secured any Building Authority's approval for construction is another story as the island's ownership is under dispute, claimed by the three cities of Hong Kong, Macau and Guangzhou; China, curiously, has not had a dog (or pig) in this fight.

24 Chinese unit of measure for food, a little over a pound.

that was by an unknown writer[25] whom the editors wished to locate, they offered to pay "a modest fee for this contribution to our journal, in any currency except the Euro which may not last beyond this century." I do wish to keep the facts as straight as possible.

Several subscribers have confirmed that they did indeed receive their catty of flying fish which, according to one enthusiastic gourmand, "awesomely delicious, flesh flaky enough when steamed to slice with chopsticks, I kept subscribing using each of my ten siblings' names just to get more fish!" It was difficult to determine how Anox+1 were able to acquire such a lot of fish. Eventually I located one Mr. Tseng, a Hong Kong taxi driver[26] and avid fisherman who confirmed that his many fishing trips with his brothers and buddies to Diaoyu (being Chinese he did not say Senkaku) always yielded an extraodinary catch. It was "as if the fish were flying to be caught." What is historically less certain is how the journal obtained money to pay writers. Subscription was free so despite the huge number of readers there was no revenue, and Anox+1 were violently opposed to courting advertisers, insisting on editorial independence unsullied by commerce. This was *possibly* (forgive this final speculation) why the publisher finally terminated publication and fired the editors and all the staff. I can confirm that for the two short book reviews and two travel pieces I contributed, I was paid a total of £55,000, which still startles me when I recall it today (or is this yesterday?). It is so rare to have your worth as a writer rewarded handsomely, and even rarer that not a single word

---

25 "Canine News" Vol 13 No 4, 2015, later republished in my book *Insignificance: Hong Kong Stories,* Signal 8 Press, 2018, which I considered a significant Hong Kong story for which I gave full credit to DD&D. Some critics still accused me of plagiarism but that is definitely fake news, so rampant these days even literary expression has fallen under its spell.

26 Tseng was born at sea into a family of boat people who were later reesettled on land, and never lost his love of fishing, often bringing home catch for dinner.

is changed by copy editors, intern readers, editors, publishers, or even accidentally by designers and their perpetual typos. Instead, every grammatical lapse, punctuation error, syntactical malfeasance, and literary illogic of your original text are preserved, which made it a wondrous publicaton to behold.

So that is a brief history of DD&D, warts, blemishes, beauty marks and all.

THE YOUNGEST CHILD

AS siblings, despite how many they were and how globally far flung, and despite their huge difference in age, they remained surprisingly close. Even though their Chinese was inflected by various accents and dialects, as well as by non-Chinese languages from all over the world, they somehow still managed to communicate. Everyone agreed their cultural centrality was remarkable, given the diverse humanity they represented, mixed as they were with all that foreign blood. Truly remarkable.

But it wasn't easy for Macau, the youngest child, who for centuries was always playing catch-up to his older siblings.

In this family of 華僑 — the Middle Kingdom's overseas branch of the family tree — Macau could rarely make himself heard. Oldest brother 大哥 always had so many stories to tell, of as many as ten or more generations — Macau was never quite sure which one was the eldest — spread all over Asia and the world as they were. One time, he called Indonesia 大家姊 which made all the older siblings laugh. Silly child, they said, you think Indonesia is the eldest sister? Hah! There were Chinese becoming *hua qiao* a lot earlier than her! A lot earlier. So who's my biggest sister then, he tried to ask, but their laughter drowned him out. Thailand 哥哥 struck a kick boxing pose and Macau tried to be brave, but of course, he knew he was no match. Stop that, 姊姊Venezuela said, don't pick on baby brother. She was the pretty one, the one with the big heart and gorgeous eyes, the one they all called Ms. World Lady. Macau was grateful for her intervention.

It was such a noisy household, everyone talking at the same time, everyone laying claim to being more truly 中. Time was never of the essence because time looped round and round the centuries as Chinese went here, there, and everywhere away from the mainland and somehow ended up very different from their ancestors back home. Even their birth order was improvisatory, like a musical composition that repeated and echoed phrases, changing as the mood dictated, even moving through different rhythms and keys. Who were their gods? The youngest child didn't know.

But now it was a new century, and all the much older siblings had settled into a kind of Chinatown immigrant and even post-immigrant life. These days, Macau only had his two immediately older brothers to pal around with, Taiwan and Hong Kong. These days, whenever Ba and Ma China lost their temper, one of the three brothers had to run and hide.

It wasn't either the best or worst of times, but it was the era of New China. Macau liked his parents' new clothes and thought Hong Kong's joke, about the emperor's new clothes, in poor taste. Taiwan was busy asserting his big brother stature and didn't pay attention to their sniping. What Macau didn't understand was why 哥哥 Hong Kong was being so mean to him lately. So he whatsapped 姊姊 Philippines who, lately, was also feeling a little sad.

I wish I weren't the baby, he texted.

You don't know how lucky you are! Youngest always the favorite.

Doesn't feel like it right now. Parents being so strict no one dares come to our casinos anymore. No more excitement and noise. Boring!

Temporary.

And why H-K-sir so nasty? H-K-sir was their shorthand for Hong Kong, although none of them dared tell him he had been so abbreviated.

Philippines pulled her long, silky hair into a ponytail. What should she say? Her baby brother was such an innocent. He didn't know how lucky he was, being a real Chinese child, unlike her, just another hybrid *huaqiao*. She thought a few minutes about his naïve outlook and finally decided that she should stop protecting him. He had to learn eventually. *It's political,* she texted. *There's nothing he can do about it but it frustrates him. So he's taking it out on you.* What she wanted to avoid was an exchange about the actual political details, all that separatist independence talk. So defiant! Sometimes, H-K-sir irritated her too. He was so stubborn, so intractable, unable to see how their parents just wanted the best for him. It was that English boarding school where he had spent far too many years. Now he thought he was another Harry Potter!

Her baby brother, however, was another story.

She decided to WhatsApp Taiwan. After all, he was more or less the oldest, at least among the real Chinese siblings, the ones their parents loved the most.

You must stop your brothers' squabbling.

What business of yours?

Baby texted. Baby was shorthand for Macau although a few of the sisters tried not to call him that, knowing he was sensitive.

The Crown Princeling! What's his problem?

He doesn't know what a star he is.

Give him time, he'll figure out. I have enough problems of my own with the parents right now. It's all CKS's fault if not for him . . .

Shh, shh, forget that he's over. Even Madame Chiang is gone now. Why dwell on the past? Right now your only concern should be the future. That's all the parents care about. No future shocks.

You're right, you're right. Taiwan felt slightly ashamed. His sister had enough problems of her own, what with that gangsta-man and his anti-China talk, and yet she was so kind towards him and the baby. He resolved to intervene and talk to his brothers today.

That night, the youngest child slept a little more soundly. It was always reassuring talking to his favorite sister because he could always count on her help. She was so good to him, like a mother. Sometimes, he wished she were his mother.

After 大哥 Taiwan talked to their brother this afternoon things calmed down a little. At least H-K-sir stopped with his Bruce Lee kicks, trying to intimidate him, and promised he would behave. He even apologized for being cranky. All because a woman had been elected to run his show! *So what?* 大哥 said. *We have one too what's wrong with women being in charge? You're just too conservative for your own good.* Later, he privately said to Macau that H-K-sir suffered from that middle-child thing, just had to be the most troublesome black sheep.

As he settled into a dream state, his eyelids getting heavier, the youngest child suddenly thought, soon it would be Chung Yeung again. Time to visit the graves, to pay respect to his ancestors. *Bom dia,* he whispered into the dark. He needed to practice his Portuguese for that day.

WHEN YOUR CITY VANISHES

IT used to be my day off, July 1. I would rise early, maybe hit the gym or meet my hiking partner for a walk through the New Territories at sunrise. Luxuriate in the empty trains of the MTR and buses that ran on time. By afternoon it was back to my rooftop room and solitude, before crowds thronged the harborside for the annual firework display.

"Because of China's nature, there is a high possibility of conflict" — Chen Po-Wei, Taiwanese lawmaker. Quoted in *The New York Times* July 1, 2020

Or did I? Who truly recalls normal life accurately during Covid-19 lockdown, when days at home seem eternal? In 2020, July 1 is political again — rousingly, noisily so, blasting global airwaves as it did back in 1997, the year that day became a public holiday in Hong Kong when my city returned to China. In case you've forgotten, my city was once the site

of "a many-splendoured thing," so titled for the novel by
Han Suyin, a Eurasian medical doctor from Shanghai who
fell in love with a married British correspondent and carried
on a controversially public affair. He died while covering
the Korean War. She wrote it as fiction — thinly disguised
autobiography — that placed my city on the world stage,
especially when glamorized as a Hollywood movie. Despite
its romantic story, the novel is a critical look at the historical,
social, and cultural problems of my Chinese city, this political
anomaly, this hybrid cosmopolitan exclave that flirts with both
East and West.

Now, "conducting with intent," as all the purple police
banners read that morning, may lead to arrest and prosecution,
an intent that's slippery in meaning— secession or subversion
— thanks to the Hong Kong Special Administrative Region's
(HKSAR) National Security Law that came into effect
after midnight of July 1, 2020. Peaceful protests are now
threatened, despite our Basic Law, just as the police now have
(and continue to gain) increasingly greater powers to arrest
people for questionably "illegal" activities. "One country two
systems," the promise, among others, that Hong Kong's rule
of law will be separate from mainland China's legal system, is
a debt of borrowed post-colonial time to retain our hybrid and
cosmopolitan way of life for 50 years, until June 30, 2047 to
be exact. That morning, however, our lender extracts a rather
large repayment, muddying the contracted time frame. Once
again, I am watching my city vanish just a little more. Trust
me, *this* is not fake news.

The flow of bounty that was Hong Kong is closing on my
vanishing city, not unlike the outdoor spigot that had to be
shut off in my northern New York home, the morning I awoke
to a flooded basement, the year Covid raged.

§

1997 used to be the flash-forward year of my childhood and early adult life. Until the early eighties, it remained that 99-year mark, the year the lease on a part of my city's land mass was due to expire on June 30. *How was it possible to rent a piece of a country,* I wondered, when this anomalous arrangement of the Convention of 1898 first entered my consciousness, a Sino-British agreement to lease the New Territories and 235 outlying islands to Britain, expanding the colonized city's territory. I think I was around nine or ten when the true meaning of Boundary Street became clear. My school was located on the north side of the street, which meant I daily crossed the border from the British colony of Hong Kong into the People's Republic of China, geographically and politically a part of the leased New Territories. How was *that* possible, my yet-to-be-decolonized mind inquired. Dad's answer was unequivocal: *this is why you do* not *want to be a colonial "British,"* although he never fully clarified why I wasn't entirely "Chinese" either — since we were Indonesian citizens — although I walked, talked, and certainly looked Chinese enough, despite my mixed blood. National affiliations are, however, difficult to ignore when I recall my passport. During the global Covid pandemic, my present document is getting a long reprieve, resting between its midnight-blue, made-in-America covers, unable to take me across borders that remain closed, forcing me to be only a virtual citizen in my city.

I never did become British, privileged as my family was to be Indonesian, although I retain my Hong Kong permanent residency. Back when I sported a dark-basil covered passport, it felt odd rather than privileged because I looked and sounded nothing like most Indonesians. There were quite a few of us foreign Asians perched in my British colony for many decades before 1997, mostly from Southeast and South Asia, as well as some from Taiwan and Vietnam. The Filipino invasion happened later, in the late eighties and early nineties, when prosperity demanded a serving class of domestic helpers. Many of us were ethnically Chinese. Among those who were not, many, myself included, spoke Cantonese like natives and several generations of these families called the city home. It was true for some British and other non-Asian nationals as well. Even though Cantonese people comprise the majority population, my Hong Kong is a city that has always looked out towards the world, this SAR that still is, and will be, for the currently foreseeable future, an exclave of China, one not entirely subject to Chinese national law. But this is changing even as I write this, and at the time of publication, it's difficult to predict how much of an exclave we will remain.

At some point, it became possible to forget about 1997. Even when Wong Kar-wai released *2046*, his excruciatingly beautiful and romantic 2005 feature film, it was all about love, obsession, and nostalgia for the way we used to be as well as the way we perhaps wish we could continue to be. In the film, 2046 is the year of a speculative, dystopic future as well as the number of a room that is unavailable for rent because a murder happened there, so the protagonist is offered room 2047 instead. Despite its apolitical drama, it is impossible to ignore the political overtones, an allusion to when our decolonized-recolonized one-country-two-systems arrangement is contracted to expire. How is it possible, the world wonders, for a country to embrace two systems within its boundaries? If you're from Hong Kong, the answer has always been blindingly crystal-clear. Once an anomaly, always an anomaly. My city is all about walking and quacking in sync with whatever power prevails.

Despite all that, July 1, 1997 remains difficult to forget. The optimists and pessimists erupted side by side on the eve of that day. Even though social media hadn't yet begun spewing its freefall lava of words and images, the world's media and intelligentsia pontificated loudly about the past, present, and future of my city during that year, the year China brought us "home." My city was like a virus, infecting global chatter for a brief moment, banging pots and pans about our fate. Dire, so dire, many experts decreed, although many others, myself included, thought differently. Memory tricks you into thinking the past is like the present, doesn't it? Yet what we think we know about life is a perpetual present tense in this deluge of knowledge, blurring conflict into a predictably repetitive cycle of *I-scream-you-scream,* like the song about ice cream, a sweet indulgence which, in the heat of the moment, melts and disappears.

In 1997, I walked through my city on the night of June 30, stopping into local parties, gliding past the Chinese ones, and witnessed Hong Kong's democracy protestors take their stand one last time under British rule. The protestors were stalwart but few that night, not of great concern to the local police. No one demanded independence or threw petrol bombs. "Foreign interference" was not evident enough for Beijing to squawk. Besides, the police had all those important dignitaries to protect from the rain, as well as crowds to control at our newly extended giant tortoise shell, the Convention Center, where the handover ceremony took place. It was at once wistful and celebratory, a good night to walk.

Now, I walk through those nights in memory, this city of mine that lends itself to long urban rambles, this city that was so safe and free of crime and disorder, this clean and orderly city where trains were graffiti-free; where universities were spaces for ideas, argument, and debate; and no one worried too much about politics or the future, because the future was always willfully rosy. Am I just a deluded flâneur of remembrance, courting nostalgia, because I, too, refuse to accept the inevitable, hoping that the way we have become is the way we will always continue to be, a future as a global Chinese exclave with a separate but equal system and culture, in the 21st century and beyond?

§

Perhaps our future can only be dreamlike, a quality that characterizes Wong Kar-wai's films. He is the filmmaker much associated with my city, one of the most well-known internationally. My father created a dream-like home in my childhood, a penthouse on the 17th and 18th floors that overlooked the Hong Kong harbor, located at the tip of Kowloon peninsula. From the verandah, it felt like I was gazing out at the world. It was an urban paradise, a home I believed would always be mine. That flat was sold years ago and our family moved to a suburban hilltop flat north of Boundary Street, one that has never felt like home to me, even though it remained in our family for almost half a century. Its rooftop room did become my 120-square-foot home for more than a decade when I lived between Hong Kong and New York, helping to care for my elderly mother with Alzheimer's until she died in 2017.

An early sign of a less-than-rosy future occurred when I was ten, the year Typhoon Dot blasted windy rainstorms. 1964 was a particularly active tropical cyclone season in the Pacific, with 39 storms recorded across the region. Dot was neither the most powerful nor the worst catastrophe in my city. 36 dead or missing and 85 people injured, all of which was bad enough but paled by comparison to Wanda, two years prior, that left 434 dead, 72,000 homeless and caused millions of dollars of damage.

But in my home Dot was catastrophic, because I awoke to an inland sea throughout both floors of our flat, on that Tuesday morning of October 13.

I was up first, as was often the case. My rubber flip flops and schoolbag floated past my bed. The water was around a foot deep. I went downstairs to the living room. Outside, a typhoon raged but the thing I *desperately* needed to know was whether or not I had to go to school. The people to ask were my maiden aunts, who lived below us on 12, facing east. From their window they could see the Royal Observatory where typhoon signals were hoisted onto a giant hilltop crucifix: black metal triangles, T's, and crosses denoting levels of severity from signals one to ten. I telephoned Aunties. Christine answered sleepily and listened to me blather on about a flood. Yes it was Signal 10, she confirmed, and no, of course there was no school. But about the water she simply snapped, *well, mop it up,* and rang off. Christine could be grumpy when dealing with kids. Only then did it dawn on me to wake my parents. Later, Mum demanded why I hadn't awakened everyone right away, but I was tongue-tied over that burning need to know about school, ashamed of my rigidly absurd view. She also complained about Christine's selfish and irresponsible response, a *what-adult-would-say-that-to-a-child* complaint. But isn't that the point of *choosing* not to be a parent, because you're not ultimately responsible for other people's children — even if you do care about them, the way Auntie Christine did love and care about our family — the way my own childlessness ensures the same?

The culprit? Wet leaves blocking the drains of our verandah, causing water to rise and seep indoors. Our penthouse flat faced south toward the open skies above the harbor, full frontal to the storm. Uprooted parquet floorboards —a foot long and approximately two inches wide — floated around like toy boats. Our family mopped all day until the typhoon dissipated and eventually vanished.

That same year, Mum finally told my sister and me, the two eldest children, that Dad was broke, his money all gone.

Our family was no longer rich with the kind of wealth that afforded my penthouse dream home. Trickle-down economics was over, and from then on, I learned to curb my enthusiasms and dreams.

In late June, just days prior to the news shock from my city on July 1, I awoke to my Northern New York basement flood on a Saturday morning. Fortunately this basement is still a concrete surface, since the contractor had mercifully not yet laid down finished tile flooring. The culprit? A likely leak in the pipes leading to the outdoor spigot that my husband and I gleefully used the previous day with our new, 100-foot hose to water our newly planted garden. By July 1, we still don't know the real cause, although the water is mopped up and a new spigot installed at the back of the house, accessible from both inside and out. The plumber closed off the line to the existing spigot, one which was inaccessible from inside unless we tore open the wall. So the flood remains a mystery of my new home, this dream home I built over five years, paid for entirely with cash from savings, investments, and earnings, while I juggled life between New York and Hong Kong. The culprit? That so-called contractor who built my new home had installed the spigot incorrectly. This engineer-project manager took my money, spent it on materials and labor but had, at best, a half-baked idea of how to build a house, being in way over his head, good intentions be damned. Even the architect gave up on him. At some point, I cut my losses and hired another, competent contractor to fix the last of his myriad and stupid mistakes.

But who will fix the "mistake" that is my city?

Was it a mistake for us to have put such faith in our promised land? By 1997, Hong Kong was prosperous. The world flocked to our shores, pouring in money, talent, visions for tomorrow. We weren't terribly worried when we first became "China" because clearly, we were still Hong Kong. I remember a young local woman, one of my sales staff at that time in my job as circulation director for the *Asian Wall Street Journal*, her face brimming with pride and joy when she spoke of the upcoming return to our Motherland. China was opening its doors to us and the world. Life was good, and we were as happy as the Clampetts in their new Beverly Hillbillies' home, funded by the Texas tea that made them rich. It's like that in TV land where reality is merely played for laughs.

Despite certain "disappearances" that occurred during the early post-Handover years, my city soldiered on. In 1997, bird flu culled 1.5 million chickens. 1998: the Asian economic crisis shrank GDP and the property market deflated by half. 1999: the first plane crash at our new airport disappeared China Airlines flight 642. 2003: SARS or Severe Acute Respiratory Syndrome, an unfortunate acronym almost identical to that of our political identity, crippled the city; meanwhile, two iconic Hong Kong pop stars, Leslie Cheung and Anita Mui, died tragically young. 2006: the demolition of the Star Ferry pier to make space for a four-lane highway. 2008: Queen's Pier, from where I used to board boats for various launch parties back in the seventies, vanished, another victim of historical erasure. By the time our city was hit by the Asian swine flu pandemic in 2009, we knew enough to shut down schools, quarantine hot spots and run temperature checks for inbound travelers.

In 2010, I returned to my city to live with my aging, Alzheimer's-stricken mother, and accepted a full-time faculty position at a local university. Prior to that, I refused to be employed full-time by any company or organization — other than by my own writing — since I'd left my 18+ year business career in 1998. I shuttled between there and my other city, New York, splitting my life between both, earning just enough from part-time employment, freelancing, and trading stocks and futures to make a life. By then, peaceful protests were the norm in Hong Kong. There was always something to complain about — no government is perfect — and every June 4, we still gathered in memory of the victims of Tiananmen, one of the few Chinese territories where commemoration was legal, although by 2021, even that's changed. The subsequent years became a personal journey through memory, retracing steps to vanished or re-imagined spaces around my city, walking across reclamations where water used to flow. I rambled often through my urban life, one that felt free, safe, reasonably democratic.

1997 became a distant memory of what had been an inevitable, historical and political reality.

But a growing concern, similar to the trepidation I later harbored towards my fake contractor, kept nudging. On July 1, 2013, thousands marched peacefully, demanding universal suffrage. It was what we'd been promised for the election of our Chief Executive as part of our Basic Law, the hallmark legal document of one country two systems. Early the next year, I employed that man — let's name him Dungeness, given his crab-like, *thick face leather* (as Cantonese 厚臉皮 articulates such shamelessness) — to design-build my rural New York home on a wooded property I had long owned; he promised to deliver my dream home. His promises were poorly fulfilled as I watched my savings dwindle. The ultimate insult was delivery of a still-unfinished, barely inhabitable house over a year behind schedule, shattering the original dream. By 2014, the Umbrella Revolution shut Hong Kong down for almost three months. By 2019, violent protests shut down more than roads and districts, and the government's rigidly absurd response signaled the beginning of the end of dreams.

§

Should we never have dared to dream?

What longing demanded I *needed* to design-build a dream home when I already owned and lived in a perfectly fine and mortgage-free raised ranch in my rural Northern New York enclave? No one *needs* more than one roof over their head. Yet over the course of my life, I have bought and sold several properties, in Hong Kong, New Zealand, and in the US in Massachusetts, Ohio, and New York, some of which were homes for a time, while others were or became rental properties. This has provided supplemental income to fund a literary life. I've also rented several homes at numerous mailing addresses — upstate New York on West Street in Lake George; Paris on the Rue St. Lazare; Greece, in Athens on Peta Street and on two islands c/o Poste Restante or American Express in Athens; an Aspen, Colorado room in the home of a coke-dealing postal worker so the mail arrived c/o her; Hamilton Avenue in Cincinnati, Ohio; New York City at Windsor Terrace, Brooklyn and Orient Avenue of Greenpoint-Williamsburg; Hong Kong in several districts — Tsimshatsui, Kowloon Tong, Shatin, Sai Kung, Causeway Bay, the Mid-Levels and the borderland between Central and Sheung Wan; Toh Street in Singapore which few taxi drivers knew existed; East College Street, Iowa City, Iowa; North 20th Avenue in Phoenix, Arizona from where I bicycled to the Valley Metro light rail. This, in addition to living for weeks or months at a stretch in hotels and writers or artists residencies. Nor does this include travel accommodations for work or pleasure, or those long stays with my English "uncle" Jack in his rose-garden cottage outside London, the year I was trying to become a real writer. Jack was a retired widower friend of Dad's, with whom he had done business during Jack's many years in Indonesia and Hong Kong. He and his wife Anne were our frequent guests at home. He offered me a free place to crash for weeks at a time to write my first novel, in exchange for cooking him Chinese meals. He even read the drafts of my novel, becoming one of my first real readers, and telegrammed me in Greece to say one of my stories had been accepted by the BBC's short story programme. It was a marvelous exchange; his generosity allowed me to dream.

Like Jack, I've led a global life, born out of a childhood in my city where the world constantly haunted our shores. Was it so wrong to dream of a home for the happily-ever-after of life? In my early twenties, I wanted a dream home in the New Territories, what was then much more rural than today. I was renting a small two-story village house in Sai Kung with my first husband, a Scotsman, where he ran a kennel for dogs on our rooftop to supplement his dog-training business. We lived well in our 1,000 square feet, across the road from the sea, where we and our own dogs — the mongrels Charley and Bloo, and the Alsatians Duke and Hera — would swim on hot summer afternoons. Both my parents grew up in villages by the sea in Central Java, and spoke fondly of the freedom of such a life. That first house did not materialize, although my family still owns the piece of village land in Taipo that my ex persuaded Mum to buy in her name, with promises of the garden she could grow there. He was persuaded by an Englishman who promised to get us a building permit, a difficult feat if you're not descended from one of the original families, a quirky problem of village property law. Dream lands, like the land in Nevada some developer persuaded Dad to buy in the desert that is still barren to this day. Our family holds title to the uninhabitable.

A few years later, I tried to build a dream home on the Greek island of Hydra where no motor vehicles are allowed, during my year in Europe and England trying to become a real writer. My then-boyfriend was an English builder who had grown up in Greece where he could work and live almost like a local, and we talked about the possibility. He also wrote wonderful letters, in his back-sloping, precise, neat handwriting, when I disappeared to Paris and London in winter, making me want to rush back to Hydra in spring. But Greece was a difficult country for a foreigner, especially a woman, to obtain building permits, never mind oversee a male construction crew. Youth dreams until life forces an awakening, and for me it was a divorce from the first husband, a break-up with the boyfriend, and ultimately, simply knowing it was time to move on and make a literary life if I ever wanted to become that real writer.

But my city already had a life! Should it be forced to "move on" from a misspent youth to become some kind of earnest grown up as a Chinese city? It was always irrevocably a part of China, we all knew that, even if we pretended for a while to be British. Had we asked to be snatched from the cradle — or was it the womb — of our motherland? Hadn't we already grown up to become a financially responsible adult, contributing wealth and investment to the motherland, alongside our playground of luxury properties, designer brands, international 5-star cuisine, a booming Chinese art market, and a springboard to the world for China's newly rich? Isn't there room enough for everyone?

Why disappear us? Why shatter our dreams?

My miscreant contractor is but a droplet in the ocean of dreams, despite shattering my self-confidence and well-being over a bad decision. My lawyer and other home builders shared stories of broken promises by contractors, which is apparently more common than not. Always over budget. Never showing up when they promise they will. Problems that should not happen in a brand new construction. The poorly installed spigot is only one in a long list of far more egregious issues, for instance failing to disclose that he had never design-built any house prior to mine, having persuaded me instead with the architect's portfolio. Disappearances. As problems and delays mounted, Dungeness routinely disappeared. Phone calls, texts, emails ignored, until he dared to come out of his locker, still believing he was justified in taking on the project. So unlike Mr. Wu, my Hong Kong contractor of many years who *always* delivered competent, professional work, on time and on budget, until he succumbed to MERS — Middle East Respiratory Syndrome — first cousin to the SARS virus, from which Covid-19, or SARS-CoV-2 evolved, and could no longer work.

However, ex-contractors, like ex-lovers or husbands, are an acceptable disappearance. It isn't the same for my city. As often as I have complained about my city — too noisy, too crowded, *way* too expensive unless you're a tycoon property developer or own numerous properties or are safely ensconced as one of the highly overpaid civil servants, tenured academics, or business executives, all who, like the three monkeys, have learned to brook no evil of sight, sound, or speech, even while evil golden-handcuffs them — I do not want this vanishing. In Hong Kong, life goes on, and the teeming masses of a lesser privilege will either shut up or die in revolution, a revolution that will have difficulty raising militia. Perhaps we should have taken a page from the Book of Mao: the Long March succeeded because it was painfully long, followed by years of deprivation, sacrifice, and want, fueled by a dream of building China's new Great Wall with "our" flesh and blood, as China's national anthem "March of the Volunteers," declares. How much more blood must my city spill before the river of red is mopped up and gone for good?

Or will our tiger economy become an increasingly toothless paper tiger, waving our Basic Law, our voices fainter and fainter as we vanish into the world's memory, scrambled by dementia, delusions, or simple forgetfulness. Who will really care if my city vanishes and the world moves on? Once a political anomaly, forever after a mistake to be rectified, so that the humiliation of the unequal treaty that gave birth to my city be disappeared forever. China rises, continues to rise, distracting the masses with all they survey in this kingdom of power and plenty. Meanwhile, the global freefall of fake and real news flows. Will *you* be able to tell the difference?

THREE

Rhododendrons

EVENTUALLY, even the rhododendrons in the corridor could not mask the smell emanating from B3. We hadn't seen him for days, but that was not unusual, not since his wife passed away earlier in the year. Letitia, the Liebermans' Filipino domestic helper, was away for her annual four-week Christmas holiday in Manila, and the morning she returned home, on December 30, she let out a shriek so loud it resonated throughout our building.

"Didn't you notice the smell?" The police asked when they came to interview us that afternoon. Apparently, Mr. Lieberman had been dead at least a fortnight, if not longer. We live in 12-A1, on the west wing of our floor facing south, and at first I was tempted to say, no, we didn't, just to stay out of the whole affair. But Mum piped up. "Stinky! Always so stinky." She glared at the policewoman, an English speaker with the red stripe on her shoulder. "That woman never throws anything away, so there are dead cockroaches and dead geckos in her piles of junk." Mum blinked, and I knew she had forgotten that Mrs. Lieberman was dead. "She's half Japanese you know. They're those Jews of China."

"Come on Mum," I said, "it's time for your bath," and I motioned to Rosa, our helper, to take my mother away. Turning to the policewoman, I switched to Cantonese: "My mother's very old and she's a bit forgetful, so don't mind what she says."

The policewoman nodded. "Did you know Mr. Lieberman well?"

"Not really. He kept to himself most of the time."

Our south-facing neighbors next to us in A2 had been

garrulous about an incident in early November and the police wanted to know if I knew who this other woman was, how they could get in touch with her and whether or not I'd seen her around recently. No, no, and no, I replied. I was glad when the hubbub finally died down that evening and we all went back to our lives behind closed doors. Now that I've crossed over into my 60s, I find too much excitement irritating, and a dead body, especially in a flat locked from the inside, is such a nuisance.

The next morning, Letitia was at our flat, jabbering away with Rosa. "Oh ma'am," she said, when I came out of my room, "it was so horrible. He was purple. And the smell! I used up two whole bottles of Dettol and it still won't go away. Even worse than sweeping up all the dead cockroaches and insects after Ma'am Lieberman died."

The police returned again, and visited all the flats on 10, 11, and 12. I gazed jealously at A3, the flat to the left of us that faced west. It was currently empty, because the Lo family were all away in California on holiday. Mr. Lo was the last corpse to leave our floor, just four months earlier, but he died of an aneurysm and there was no mention of foul play. Mrs. Lieberman had expired at home in B-3 after a long illness, and was the corpse back in March prior to Mr. Lo. And B-1 and B-2 were not really part of our floor, because those were the upstairs of the joined penthouse flats on 11, so their doors remained perpetually locked. I'd never seen them once in the decade since they moved in. Which left the Chans in A2 next door to us, whose dog barked furiously every time I came home, and who had been barking even more furiously in November during the incident of the woman in the corridor.

She was from China, surnamed Zhang, Rosa said, and was Mr. L's current lover. Now, with both Rosa and Letitia having tea in our living room, I heard the entire story again.

"I bet she murdered him, ma'am, because he wouldn't sell the flat and give her the money. A million dollars he gave her already, and still she wanted more. You should have heard her, screaming away outside our door. Mr. L refused to let her in and she finally went down to the lobby and then after he went out, she came back up and forced her way in past me and broke those porcelain pigs and rabbits Mrs. L brought from their home in Shanghai." Letitia took a deep breath. "Poor Ma'am L, those were her favorites. Mr. L didn't even wait for his ma'am to die to take this woman as a girlfriend. They've been together at least two years. I warned him she was trouble. His son in Shanghai also warned him, but men, what can you say? And now he's dead. Murdered!"

It didn't seem likely to me, but by now, the whole building was talking about the murdered Jew in 12 A-3.

Rosa chimed in. "I thought Jews were very smart. How come he was so stupid to fall for this crazy woman?"

I refused to fuel further speculation, and murmured something about Jews being people like everyone else, some were smart and others not. The building was as abuzz as it had been years earlier in 1973, when Bruce Lee died here, on 3, if I recall correctly, although it wasn't a murder that time, just cerebral edema while he was with his lover. I wasn't so sure it was murder now, but with the police traipsing in and out of the flat down the hall, it was hard not to be swept up by all the talk and excitement. Letitia had worked for the Liebermans for twenty years, but I remember their arrival, thirty years earlier, when Dad was still alive and chatted with them regularly, although Mum remained guarded and suspicious, the way she was with everyone in our building. Dad and the Indian family on 10 were probably the only ones, besides the Filipino domestics, who spoke to the Liebermans, and somehow, I didn't think it was murder, even if the evidence, or rather the gossip, pointed to that possibility.

Our family had moved to Hong Kong from Jakarta in the late '60s when I was in high school. We used to rent over on the island, in Causeway Bay, close to the Indonesian Consulate. We bought our flat in this building when it was first built back in 1970, on this hilltop in Kowloon Tong, and this has really been my home in Hong Kong. Back then we and the Indians on 10 were the only foreigners here. So when the Liebermans arrived, I welcomed the added diversity. By then I had graduated from university and was working for the Hongkong & Shanghai Bank. It's HSBC now and is where I still work in private banking.

"The Jews of China," Dad had declared over dinner one night, "are like us wah kiu in Southeast Asia. The professionals and the traders, we Chinese Jews make money and believe in education." It was shortly after the Liebermans moved in. Their son was around ten or so at the time, a likable boy and who had, like his parents, reddish hair.

Mum ignored his declaration. "How come they have red hair?"

"They're Ashkenazi Jews," I said. "Some have red hair."

"And how come she's part Japanese?"

By now, Dad was fiddling with the television channels and was no longer paying attention to anything Mum said.

"People marry and have children, Mum. Even the Japanese and Jews."

"They're so strange."

Dad didn't find them strange at all, and he often came home with stories about Mrs. L's rhododendrons. There were at least a dozen pots of the colorful fragrant blooms in the hallway and even after her death, Mr. L kept them there and Letitia watered each pot faithfully. Mrs. L had originally asked Dad if it was okay for her to place her rhododendrons in the corridor, for the southern light from the windows at the lift, she said, to which Dad said why not. Mum was livid and nagged him for weeks after that, saying our Cantonese neighbors wouldn't like it and why did he have to tell her that? Later, she complained to me that Dad was flirting again.

Back then, Dad worked from home, while Mum and I went out to work. It was true that Dad was very friendly with Mrs. L. They both liked music and talked about opera all the time. Sometimes I would come home from work and find them both listening to opera on Dad's stereo. Our large crystal vase in the living rooms would be full of rhododendrons whenever she visited. I wondered if Mr. L minded, but whenever I saw him, he was always pleasant and complimented my appearance, asking, why didn't I have a boyfriend. He definitely had an eye for Chinese women. He gave me a pretty porcelain vase as a gift one Chinese New Year. I still have it.

I remembered all that now in the wake of Mr. L's demise. It was all hearsay, but he apparently had choked to death, although it wasn't clear if someone strangled him. But the crazy woman who created the huge ruckus didn't have a key to the flat, of that Letitia was absolutely positive. Even if she was jealous of Mrs. L, and later, Letitia as well, it didn't necessarily mean she killed him, especially if she had no way into the flat. Rosa heard some talk among the other Filipino helpers about a fish bone, but later that turned into a chicken bone, and still later someone said he had coughed up a lot of blood.

Yet the police were in and out of our building for days.

Madam Policewoman and a young assistant showed up a week later with more questions for me. "There aren't many Jewish people living around here, are there?"

I wondered what the point was, but simply assented, saying nothing.

"Why did they live here so long?"

Here it was again, the local attitude about anyone different. I passed as local because I spoke Cantonese, and these days, even Mandarin fluently, although my parents had never quite mastered the local languages and defaulted to English. But it was tiresome, how much the locals missed. About everything.

"It was their home. Mr. Lieberman had an import and export business in Chinese porcelain, and their son went to school here in Kowloon Tong." She looked dubious, so I added, "They're from Shanghai, but have been in Hong Kong since the fifties."

"Really?" She looked sincerely startled.

"Really." Hoping to deflect further questions, I asked if they'd found the Chinese woman, surnamed Zhang.

"Yes. She says she hasn't been near the building in days. Have you seen her around?"

In fact, I had seen her lurking in the lobby a couple of days earlier, and wandering around the car park where she stopped next to Mr. L's car. Letitia said she often waited around, hoping to catch him when he went out.

"I don't recall," I replied.

"He had red hair. It's strange don't you think?"

Enough, I thought. I made some excuse about having to see to my mother and dismissed her as soon as I could.

This year has been unusual, with all these corpses leaving our building. The elderly Indian lady on 10 passed away at the beginning of the year as well. She was one of the last, besides my mother, who made it into their 90s. Mr. Lo was an aberration, an undiagnosed abdominal aneurysm, his daughter said. He was in his 60s, like me. Most of our neighbors now are younger families, like the Chans next door with their noisy mutt. The Liebermans were in their 70s. She had been a packrat for some time, and when she died, the mountains of newspapers and magazines she hoarded disappeared even before her body was cold. I couldn't blame Mr. L, though. From what Letitia told us, it was all she could do to eke out a pathway between the heaps of rubbish in order to do some semblance of cleaning. It was no wonder he stayed out so much, and I could almost even forgive him his woman from China, surnamed Zhang. She was crazy but sexy, with wild hair and eyes. And Mrs. L had been ill for almost three years, virtually bedridden.

It was different when Dad died ten years earlier. By then he flirted openly with Mrs. L, and every afternoon, they took a walk together before dinner in the park below. So I had to listen to Mum berate him at dinner every night, on and on about how could he behave like that, how could he humiliate her like that, until I learned to tune it out. By then, Mum's memory was in partial decline, and Mr. L was screwing around although that was a different woman, from Taiwan, surnamed Chao. She was at least sane and didn't show up at our building. Letitia told Rosa that he kept her in a flat on the island.

The police came the time Dad died as well, because his death occurred at home, so that was standard procedure. By the time they arrived, I had flushed the remains of the mixed-up medication Mum fed him. She had been a pharmacist, and even though her memory had begun to fail, she still knew what she was doing. Dad had a weak heart, and took a whole bunch of different medications which Mum administered, so it was easy for her to give him too much of something to trigger the attack. I could never be sure but I'm more inclined to believe that if there was a murder in our building, it was Dad who was the victim and not Mr. L (or Bruce Lee for that matter, because that's been thoroughly picked over by history). Mum was so distraught. She found Dad in bed, dead, when she came home after morning mass. I spoke to the police for Mum and they only came to see us twice, and at the hospital they simply wrote it off as death by heart attack with a precondition of a weak heart.

So why is it the police are still here two weeks later, hounding us with endless questions about these Jews in our building? What is it they really expect to learn? Can't they just let Mr. L rest in peace? You'd think they'd never seen a Jewish person before, but…that might well be the case. I suppose it helps that we look Chinese, despite our mixed Indonesian blood. Maybe it's the red hair. Really, it's all just too strange.

背景 THE VIEW FROM 2010

IN 2010, the second morning of the Year of the Pig is the day after Valentine's. Hong Kong's in a good mood. On ATV Home, Harmony News broadcasts a senior citizen activity organized by a Christian social welfare group. Its goal—to reproduce past times by displaying personal possessions these seniors have preserved and stag ing pop songs and dances they perform, sporting makeup, wigs, and clothing from their youth. One woman could still wear her wedding dress.

Today, ATV no longer exists, this free-to-air television station with two language channels—Cantonese Home and English World. The station died on April 1, 2016, its license renewal denied by the Hong Kong government. Home couldn't compete with more commercially popular TVB Jade, though World gave TVB Pearl a run for its money. ATV World was perhaps too good at broadcasting all our news in English, the global language, news too readily re-broadcast worldwide, because by 2016, protests in my city had grown louder, and discontents simmered to a dangerous boil.

But on the second day of that Pig year, I am watching Home because mornings are when I catch up on local news, harmonious or contentious, in Cantonese, the language of my city's heart. Our minority language, English, has less to say locally in the mornings, and the Anglo channels — CNN, BBC, Australian Broadcasting, as well as France 24, NHK, Arirang, Al Jazeera, DW — all that foreign media have fewer correspondents than in days of yore, when Britannia still ruled the waves, and us.

It's impossible, if not heretical, to consider my city today without that "view from behind" of our 背景, as Chinese articulates a background or backstory. In February, 2010, I move home once again to live in my birth city; it's the last time I'll do so. My personal 背景 of cour age, cowardice, and compromise is this insider's entry path to reflect on our chaotic present.

It takes courage for protestors to wave the British flag in 2019, when the world is witnessing the largest and most prolonged protests by the citizenry, some of whom perpetrate the worst violence in Hong Kong's history. Nineteenth-century gunboat diplomacy—how unequal treaties were signed in favor of the colonizer—seems tame by comparison. Is it Dutch courage or true heroism Grandma Wong displays, this sixty-plus-year-old who consistently appears, wielding a large Union Jack? She will not compromise: Hong Kong under England, she claims, had a future. Many protestors do not agree; as a colonized people, we *were* second-class citizens. Likewise, the courageous minorities on different spectrums—those demanding independence, freed of Chinese rule; those resorting to violence, risking arrest, because only then will they not be ignored—they, too, cannot compromise. Most protestors disagree, but the more recalcitrant the local government's stance, in line with China's unwillingness to ac cede to demands for greater democracy, the more likely the protests and strikes will be prolonged, with perhaps more violence and even louder cries for independence.

The ball is in the Hong Kong Government's court, more than it's ever been in the history of our city, and they must find the right compromise. It troubles me to see such outrage in our streets, grassroots courage, a courage that should have manifested much earlier in our short history. To mount a real revolution, as opposed to the polite tea parties[27] of Hong

---

27 "A revolution is not a dinner party, or writing an essay, or painting a picture, or doing embroidery; it cannot be so refined, so leisurely and gentle, so temperate, kind, courteous, restrained, and magnanimous. A revolution is an insurrection, an act of violence by which one class overthrows another." — Mao Zedong

Kong's numerous protest marches. The Chairman knew: revolution was the Long March, bloodshed and sacrifice, something Hong Kong's youth are finally discovering late, too late.

Should I have had the courage to abandon my family and city when I was younger, as young as many of these protestors are today? In the journey of my private revolution, I, too, did not find courage soon enough to completely transform my life.

I left Hong Kong for good in the fall of 2018. Since my first departure at the age of seventeen, it's been a lifelong shuttle, mostly between New York and Hong Kong, in my quest to live an independent, creative life as an English-language writer. My secret desire was to be a traitor to my origins, *especially* to acceptance of Confucian filial piety, to become "the writer" as a migrant to the West. It was what American author Ha Jin has named his own linguistic and nationalistic "betrayal."

In November, 2017, my mother died shortly before her ninety-eighth birthday. By then, my former position as writer-in-residence at a local university had also died. Meanwhile, my husband-to-be was still patiently waiting back home in New York after our seven-year, long-distance relationship, while I squatted "at home" in Hong Kong with Mum's debilitating Alzheimer's. Our homes in Manhattan and Northern New York beckoned. Clean air, space, affordable life, and love felt like the more desirable way to enter senior citizenship than perching, precariously, in the overpriced, overcrowded, over-enervated space that was my city. We were mortgage-free, and New York City still recognized my husband's rent-stabilized apartment in what was, by now, the fashionable Chelsea Meatpacking District in which he first squatted back in the 1980s, when few others would venture west. By 2019, I would even be eligible for Medicare. What more could a migrant writer want?

Then, summer arrived, and Hong Kong was besieged by another internationally newsworthy moment, shattering my optimistic calm.

It was 1989 all over again, when tanks rolled into Tiananmen Square on June 4. That was the last time an equivalent-sized crowd in Hong Kong marched in protest. Then, I had looked on from my home in Brooklyn, New York, glued to the news, weeping, frustrated, and help less. We were not yet under China's rule but knew that within a decade we would be. Yet despite Tiananmen, Hong Kong remained hopeful. To protest was still our lawful right, and in the years that followed, the annual vigils at Victoria Park ensured *luhk sei*, 6-4, our moniker for Tiananmen, would not be forgotten, unlike the revisionist history that prevailed on the Chinese mainland.

In 2010, it startles me how many young mainlanders studying at our universities as "foreign" students will, for the first time, learn this history; even so, some remain skepti cal, convinced as they are by the erasure of what they have *not* learned. But from '89 onward, such amnesia would not be the case in Hong Kong, this soon-to-be-former British colony, one of the last postcolonials, and the first to be named a Chinese Special Administrative Region under our dubiously unique "one country, two systems" arrangement, with its own Basic Law. We would not and did not forget.

A few years after Tiananmen, in the summer of '92, I had moved back to Hong Kong to live. What hope we had then! The economy was thriving, the future was promising, and the dire predictions of PLA tanks rolling into the city on July 1, 1997, the day we were to be handed back to China was, as any local knew, alarmist reportage by misguided Western media.

The West did misread that moment we became part of

China again, as documented in my novel *The Unwalled City*. In the early years after the handover, things did not seem dire. We survived the Asian Economic Crisis that erupted a year later, because our city's culture is really *the economy, stupid,* an apt anthem to our deeply pragmatic, mercantile nature. W. H. Auden poetically observed this of our city when visiting in 1938, noting that *Here in the East the bankers have erected / A worthy temple to the Comic Muse.* He did however conclude that *For what we* (England) *are, we have ourselves to blame.* The city's sheen, it seems, has long disoriented visitors: they fall in love with the surface but remain puzzled by our soul. Local scholar Stuart Christie elaborates on Auden's visit thus: "Hong Kong is not, in the end, where poets come to be remembered; it is a place of final retreat where, fleeing a reality they can neither fully transcribe nor fully comprehend, they must disembark."

And in 2010, whether or not we share Auden's particular disorientation, which Christie attributes in part to his gaze as a gay man, Hong Kong is still a disorienting space: cosmopolitan, glitzy, and frustrating for serious writers. Yet it's also safe, efficient, clean, and more accessible for literary endeavors in ways that would be harder in London or New York. A hybrid culture has evolved, one that is peculiarly apolitical but prescient in its view of the future of humanity. While much of our literature is naturally influenced by our Chinese origins, we are not completely tied to the history, culture, geography, or even language of our sovereign ruler. In fact, local writers look to the world, China included, for ideas, images, inspiration, while still retaining a deep-rooted sense of Hong Kong's own identity and nature. Which is why, in 2010, I agree to create Asia's first low-residency MFA in creative writing at a local public university. We are a space that writers of all ethnicities, origins, and native tongues can *choose* to express themselves in English, the world's lingua franca, even while questioning the imperialist influence of that language in global publishing.

I used to be able to think in terms of a rod or furlong as units of measure and do sums in pounds, shillings, and pence. I knew how much a guinea or farthing was, and the correct pronunciation for ha'penny and thrupence. That was in the distant realm of a colonial childhood in Hong Kong, which, for me, is over half a century ago. Yet fifty years is as long as or even longer than five hundred in China's recent past, a country whose earliest recorded *written* history dates back to 1250 BCE. Its real history goes back even earlier.

So perhaps it's not so startling to learn that a kilogram is no longer what it used to be? On my fifty-seventh birthday, *The Economist* re ports the kilogram is "the last bit of the International Systems of Units (SI) to be tied explicitly to an artefact." By 2010, I have begun reading *The Economist* to remind myself that in some of my world, "artifact" is spelled "artefact," in part to counter the US-centric worldview that dominates the Anglophone world where I live. A not-always-happy resident in an America where my space is relegated to "immigrant writing." I do not write immigrant narratives like Amy Tan or Max ine Hong Kingston, but in New York of the '80s and '90s, there was little space for a transnational or global Asian voice. Far more space was given to the white male writer who helicoptered into my city, who perpetuated every cliché and stereotype, who only articulated the surface and ignored our soul. By 2010, I no longer tolerate such nonsense and would rather contribute to broadening an Anglophone literary space with Asian, and Hong Kong, characteristics.

How did it happen, this time collapse?

Hong Kong has never been overly fond of its own history.

For years, our history was recorded by the British, who told it from their perspective. Now, China will record our history, to ensure the unequal treaty that gave birth to our city will never be forgotten. However, Chinese history has long been taught in local schools, even during the colonial era, a curriculum which local historian Flora L.F. Kan describes as "a Han-centered cultural view." School curricula, she notes "does not support theories of colonial cultural imperialism, in which colonial governments dictate the nature of school curricula in order to diminish the culture of the local population" (3). After the hando ver, Hong Kong history was even included "as an appendix to the official syllabus" (136-7). But she concludes that "at the classroom level, teachers have not given much attention to national identification" and that while the teaching "continued to adhere to Han-centered interpretations of Chinese history, moral and civic education seem to be taken less seriously" (137).

It is difficult, if not impossible, to grow up in Hong Kong and attend a local school without learning how Chinese you are. This was true even for me, a *wah kiu* whose overseas Chinese parents migrated from Indonesia, and whose identity was foreign because we had Indonesian, rather than Hong Kong British, citizenship as well as some Indonesian blood. Even though I did not study Chinese history beyond the primary level and defected to an English-only curriculum in secondary, as "foreigners" like myself did, I still understood, deeply, what it meant to be Chinese.

And part of being Chinese is to feel the pull of the motherland, no matter where in the world you live.

It's a false positive, this cultural heartstring, one the Chinese Government propagates into a tyranny of nationalist love for the nation or 愛國.

We never became truly postcolonial, because we were

always too cowardly, or too compromised, to overthrow our oppressor. Picture a revolution in the 1960s for Hong Kong's independence, one begun by its own citizens. This would have been during the Cultural Revolution, when China had enough problems of its own. What would China have done if two million people marched through our streets, demanding the overthrow of Britain? What would Britain have done? Shortly after 2010, the world learns from documents released by the UK's National Archives, that Britain contemplated implementing self-governance as early as the 1950s, but that China threatened to invade if Britain did so, preferring the colonial status quo. Instead, our most significant protest was the 1967 riots, a leftist uprising against the British that erupted on our shores. Most Hong Kongers opposed the violence. The local riot police were sent to quell unrest and British forces defused around eight thousand home-made bombs. In the end, the bombings by the leftists were defused by then Chinese premier Zhou Enlai, who issued them an order to stop. It lasted eighteen months, but peace was restored.

The problem was, Britain was just not oppressive enough, and the locals just didn't care enough to foment revolution when there was work, education, and abundant opportunity, especially for those willing to sacrifice themselves for the next generation. Who really cared about snobbish Brits in their tony enclaves on Hong Kong Island, up on the Peak, say, or who hogged the south shore's seafronts? The rest of us teemed over on the peninsula of Kowloon and the New Territories, relegating the white man to his ghostly realm, the *gweilo* who was not really human. Racism in a colony is a two-way street.

The *real* problem was, we were never Chinese enough, not the way over a billion Chinese in the motherland are.

Was it cowardice on our part to shirk independence and instead strive to become rich, gloriously so, by remaining second-class Brits?

To get rich is glorious, the phrase generally attributed to Deng Xiaoping may, after all, be fake news popularized by Western media (there is no definitive proof he actually said this), so we cannot claim that our future sovereign leader told us so. Was it cowardice the local elite displayed, buying their way out of a Communist future by securing passports from Australia, Canada, Britain, and the United States, transforming their children into lost boys and girls? All those ABCs, BBCs, CBCs et al who would rather come home to cushy Hong Kong, with live-in maids to cook and clean for them, Mummy and Daddy to house them, friends to play with who live the way they do, code-mixing languages and cultures? Home where, above all, they need not feel displaced in their capitalist paradise? The exodus of foreign-passport-seekers became the rhythm of our history: after 1967, 1982, 1989, and 1997.[28]

The twenty-first century initially saw fewer departures. Those who leave are likely driven more by the economic inequities that make the city unaffordable and the teeming population that is currently projected to swell to almost 7.8 million makes the city a less desirable habitat in which to imagine a future. In the twenty-first century, some have moved north to the mainland, unlike in the past, because opportunity, space, affordable housing, and schooling in Chinese, or readily available international schooling for the elite, beckoned. Speaking Mandarin was easier on the tongue than English, and at least you looked like everyone else. Hong Kong people, as the Chinese government likes to say, *are* Chinese.

But in 2014, the Umbrella Movement closed down the city, and the then CEO panicked, ordered police out with tear gas, was too cowardly to face the students. Instead he sent his deputy, Carrie Lam Cheng Yuet-ngor, the current CEO who,

---

28 1967: the leftist riots; 1982: the joint declaration between the United Kingdom and China to return Hong Kong to Chinese sovereignty; 1989: Tiananmen; 1997: the handover.

in 2019, presides over a more disruptive and far more violent protest—one the Centre for Global Research, alongside Chinese media, says is sponsored by the U.S. The world is enamored of fake news made to appear so real it virtually becomes real, this phenomenon invented and promulgated by the current American president.

It's the compromises that trip you up. In 2010, I do not want to go home. Instead I'd rather continue dinging between New York and Hong Kong. I had left the city "for good" once before in '98, to live with my lover in Manhattan. By 2010, we have a long history, and I teach at a college in Vermont where I've recently been elected faculty chair at a long-established low-residency MFA. Inhabiting flight paths has become my way of life.

It's the discontents of being transnational that trip you up. This unsolicited offer to start Asia's first low-residency MFA in writing promises more money than any college in the United States could match. Can I do it part-time, I ask, the way it is at all low-residency programs? Can I continue my life between two cities? Can I, essentially, have the best of all my worlds? No, no, and no, they reply. I have never been a full-time academic, never desired that career, and the move is daunting. Yet the prospect of creating a writing program that speaks to the kind of writer I am—can I really turn that down?

Besides, Mum *needs* someone to live at home with her.

Thomas Wolfe warned: *you can't go home again.* Those who tried were rarely content. My private library bears witness to that truth, all those words by writers who shaped and influenced my own voice: Marguerite Duras, Han Suyin, Vladimir Nabokov, Doris Lessing, Joseph Conrad, Somerset Maugham, Lu Xun, John Cheever, Andre Dubus, Thomas Wolfe, Graham Greene, Gao Xingjiang, F. Scott Fitzgerald, Shirley Jackson,

Anna Kavan, Katherine Mansfield, Janet Frame, Maxine Hong Kingston, Derek Walcott, Zhang Kangkang, Mo Yan, Ding Ling, Jonathan Swift, Shawn Wong. They, however, are already a part of my history of becoming a writer, and recent immersion has been in writerly minds and hearts that speak more closely to my own lived experiences and musings: Sharmistha Mohanty, Pico Iyer, Kwame Anthony Appiah, Ha Jin, Bino Realuyo, Tina Chang, Luis Francia, Robin Hemley, James Scudamore, Jill Dawson, Ira Sukrungruang, Sybil Baker, Tash Aw, Evan Fallenberg, Marilyn Chin, Yan Geling, Tabish Khair, Lasana Sekou, Kwame Dawes, Madeleine Thien, Jess Row, Rawi Hage, Rigoberto Gonzales, among others. Plus there's all that Hong Kong Anglo literary culture, of which I was an early pioneer, even co-editing two anthologies of Hong Kong writing in English for a local university press in the early '00s. I became a reluctant scholar just to prove that yes, a literature of Hong Kong does and *should* exist.

So shouldn't I also simply surrender to the Chinese obligation of filial piety and go home to look after Mum? By then her Alzheimer's diagnosis is definite. I am both eldest and 大家姐.[29] My three younger siblings will only step in if I shirk my familial role. Mum's voice booms from my distant past, decibels louder than all the noise of my selfish literary past (a career path that is anathema to any Hong Kong parent): *you must be a good example for your younger sisters and brother.* If you're Chinese, truly Chinese, you just *know*— family responsibility outranks individual dreams, every time.

Even though you can't go home again, I went home to live at twenty, briefly at twenty-seven, again at thirty-eight, and disappeared for what was to have been the last time at the age of forty-four. So there I was, at fifty-six, vacil lating once again,

---

29 Literally, "big sister of the family."

trying to decide. What *else* could I do? I went home. The young protestors today are not such compromised souls. It's the older generations—mine and those a decade or so younger— who juggled cowardice and compromise as citizens of Hong Kong. Financial security, and in some cases wealth, is the cowardly artist's pushback against "suffering" for art, suffering often celebrated in the West. Although when I look around New York publishing today, I doubt that was ever truly the case. Likewise, to have demanded independence from the British was our *least* likely path. In particular, we university-educated were catapulted into the privilege of good jobs, careers with futures, affordable domestic help (especially for families with children), property prices that soared in the decades ahead mak ing us asset-rich. Even those "astronauts" of the '80s who landed in Vancouver and elsewhere, squatting long enough for a foreign passport, came home. Our city had become first world by the '90s, and elsewhere looked more impoverished, inefficient, crime-ridden, and unfriendly by comparison. Although inflation shot property prices through the roof, our salaries kept pace. Most important, government and industries were rapidly "localizing"—the white man no longer reigned supreme. We had our moment and could nurture a belief in our Hong Kong identity and reality.

What surprised the world, and us, was the rapidity of the rise of China.

It is strange today to reflect on that surprise. After all, China's history is one of perpetual transformation from one dynasty to the next, and the only way for its economy to head was up. It also had a population hungry for change. In the early to mid '00s, I contemplated living in Beijing. The city was spacious and still affordable, I could improve my Mandarin, the ethos was less consumerist than in Hong Kong, and literature was rooted in its own worldview and aesthetic, without the obeisance to the West that still marked Hong Kong. China was opening up to the world and there was a curiosity, and openness, among people I met. A cultural heart that was missing in my own city, where money mattered above all else. Besides, China was huge, like America, and no one ethos really ruled supreme, while Hong Kong was tiny, insular, and too restrictively self-satisfied.

By 2010, Beijing is beginning to feel less attractive, but each time I go to the mainland, mostly to Shanghai or Beijing, there's still enough to like. In fact, Hong Kong students who shun those from China seem small-minded, mean, and short-sighted.

However, the greatest shock to the system is when Hong Kong itself begins to change. It starts from within, and not just as a result of edicts issued by Beijing. Our elites—the industrialists, property magnates, academics[30], and government officials—the ones who earn the highest salaries and perch on the peak of the economic pyramid, they feather their nests and either fly the coop or nestle into cozier, lucrative nests up north offered by China, with little regard for Hong Kong's well-being.

As a full-time academic for the first time, I witness the worst corruption and waste of my entire professional career. I have written elsewhere of this experience, centered on the program I directed, which was shut down in 2015 for the most frivolous of reasons.[31] I realize my view from 2010 is distorted by rose-colored lenses: Hong Kong's future will not be nearly

30 Hong Kong university professors, in all disciplines, are among the highest paid in the world, their salary scale linked to that of the civil service. Notably, the Chief Executive of Hong Kong earns more than the President of the United States.
31 In my memoir *Dear Hong Kong: An Elegy for a City* (Penguin, 2017), I write about the controversial and bumbling closure of the MFA program, a move often viewed as politically motivated, despite the university's denial. Also see https://www.facebook.com/ SaveCityUMFA?fref=ts

so rosy. Time doesn't heal *all* wounds, it only clarifies why you hurt in the first place.

In 2014, a legislative misstep launched the Umbrella Movement, further compounded in 2019 by a second legislative misstep.[32] Hong Kong has become a cauldron of discontent, waiting to erupt if provoked.

Yet what shocked me most, when the Umbrella Movement derailed the city, was how *little* empathy there was for the protestors among the majority of Hong Kongers. Admittedly, the message was muddled, this tea party revolution that was, for the most part, civilized and peaceful, respectful of the rule of law. The outpouring by so many writers, artists, actors, singers, and photographers was heartening, even if it all felt too sweet and naïve. A jarring recall from '67—while watching the protests in the streets, I wondered why my city felt so precarious and temporary.[33]

Nothing much changed after the Umbrella protestors packed up and left, but what was palpable were the rumblings of discontent in the months afterwards. A rise in crime. Property prices soaring to absurd heights. The further erosion of freedom of speech. A shrinkage of meaningful jobs and salaries for school leavers and college grads. Growth of a population living at or below the poverty level. The ongoing battle between mainlanders and locals, whether those from China were tourists, migrants, or wealthy investors.

It was like reverting to the '60s all over again, when I had

32 In 2014, the decision by Beijing for proposed electoral reforms to achieve universal suffrage in the city was seen as undemocratic and restrictive, because the candidates would essentially be pre-selected and approved by the Chinese Government. In 2019, a proposed extradition law was widely opposed because it meant China could extradite anyone in Hong Kong to the mainland to be tried and sentenced under Chinese law.
33 See "Democracy," a short story set during the '67 riots in my collection *History's Fiction: Stories from the City of Hong Kong*, 1st ed., Chameleon Press, 2001.

edged into puberty and wanted nothing more than to leave the purgatory of home.

In 1965, I was eleven and published my first creative piece in the children's section of the leading English-language newspaper. Besides my immediate family, and one Danish school friend, no one remarked this achievement. In time, I would come to see my writing as a secret, underground activity, one that had no reality in Hong Kong because it was in the wrong language, and I had the wrong color skin. Through Girl Guides and other inter-school activities, I would meet English school students who presented an alternative local world.

But Britain struck me as the wrong country to gaze at with much longing, despite its literary appeal. Instead, I trained my sights elsewhere. There was so much to distract—all that jazz, Motown, the Doors, Barbara Streisand, Aretha Franklin, Diana Ross, TV, movies, even some American literature, Mark Twain, say, or those nineteenth-century Gothics, Nathaniel Hawthorne and Edgar Allen Poe. Later, Woodstock, all that delectable noise, coupled with a moon landing. The promise of a country where many, many freedoms and possibilities unfolded, a young country, built by migrants from many nations.

Meanwhile, my city was filthy and crime-ridden, corruption was rampant (Mum was constantly bribing *someone*), the education system was stiflingly rote, leading to public exams, exams, and more exams, followed by suicides of those who failed to pass with high enough marks, bringing shame to their family. It was so disgustingly Chinese, this punishing class and value system where the elite—wealthy Cantonese and Shanghainese—ruled, alongside the Brits who wanted nothing to do with us less-celestial folk. I craved a high school like Clark Kent's in Smallville and to jeer at the establishment the way *Mad Magazine* did. *Mad's* lyrics to *The*

Sound of Music—dough, means cash, for all of us—such freedom to excoriate American capitalism, Hollywood, and mindless entertainment! Clark Kent appealed. He, like me, harbored a secret and was an alien who did not belong on Earth, just as I did not really belong in Hong Kong.

In 2018, as I watched my city eject a *Financial Times* journalist for giving Andy Chan Ho-tin, founder of the Hong Kong National Party and a pro-independence activist, a forum to speak at the Foreign Correspondents Club, I did not regret my decision to leave for good.

It's August, and the summer of 2019 is sizzling the planet. I am grateful not to be in Hong Kong, where the heat would be unbearable amid overbuilt concrete. A notice for an arts event "back home," *Consciously Unconscious,* pings my inbox. This is apparently a series of interviews with leading artists in Hong Kong through images, insights, and reflections to take us to "the personal heart of creativity and its centrality in life." Has Hong Kong been for too long consciously unconscious of its very self, in denial that its future is doubly and triply mortgaged? The violence, protests, and anger erupt weekly, even daily, while life (and art) goes blissfully on.

Recently, the BBC interviewed me on World Update[34] about the protests, wanting the viewpoint of an insider who had spent the greater part of her adult life in Hong Kong. And once again I found myself sad, as sad as I was in 2014 when I watched my crying city protest in its courteous, restrained, magnanimous, and *futile* manner. A long banner that hung from an overpass read 父姆為我哭 了 我為將來哭了 with the translation *Our parents are crying for us. I am crying for the future.*[35]

34 BBC World Update July 30, 2019.
35 Xu:"The Crying City" *Bellingham Review,* Spring 2016. 53-61; also col lected in Xu: *This Fish is Fowl,* Nebraska University Press, 2019. 67-78.

I do not want today's protests to also be for naught. I almost wish an independence party would emerge, in exile, even if independence is not what most people want. Opposition means the fighting spirit from my city will not die. Earlier this year, the Hong Kong Government objected to Germany granting political asylum to two activists. History swaps one dictator for another, in its never-ending cycle of repeating itself. After all, America looks a lot less like the country I once admired from afar, in the innocence of my Hong Kong youth.

Despite my exit from the city of my birth,[36] my extradition is likely not final. There is always hope that one may return, that home will somehow still be there, even if the decor has changed. From a once barren rock to a world city to a future as a Chinese city... in the end, will it take Hong Kong's pragmatically mercantile soul, plus a hybrid form of courage that endures second-class citizenship, to shape its identity and ensure its survival?

---

36 The city I've described as the "pimple on the backside of China" in *Evanescent Isles: from my city-village,* Hong Kong University Press, 2004.

Works Cited

Auden, W. H. "Hongkong." *Collected Poems*. Ed. E. Mendelsen. Vintage Books, 1991.

Cartalucci, Tony. "US Sponsored 'Color Revolution' Struggles in Hong Kong," *Global Research*, June 27, 2019. https://www.globalresearch.ca/us-color-   revolution-struggles-hong-kong/5681898

Christie, Stuart. "Disorientations: Canon without Context in Auden's Sonnets from China": *PMLA* Volume 120, Number 5, October 2005, pp 1576-1587.

Jin, Ha. *The Writer as Migrant*. University of Chicago Press, 2008.

Kan, Flora L.F. *Hong Kong's Chinese History Curricula from 1945: Politics and Identity* Hong Kong University Press, 2007.

Xu Xi. *The Unwalled City*. Chameleon Press, 2001.

Lightning

AFTERWARDS, everyone spoke of speed. That slanted flash, like a chef's rapid flickflack blade. Filleting a fish, butterflying a steak. It razed the plane at an angle, cleanly through the fuselage.

The plane had just ascended, inclined 25 degrees after liftoff. The bolt from the blue split it open. Engine and fore cabin in flames. Bodies fell, a few charred beyond recognition. Some died as much from fright as from injury. All three of the flight crew, lived.

That drizzly Tuesday afternoon in the summer of '68, she saw the whole thing from the outdoor observation deck at Kai Tak. No one was out there to witness either her private heartbreak or the murderous flash. She was seeing off her lover, or rather, seeing off his plane. He, on board with his wife headed home to Connecticut, he perished but the wife survived, crippled for life.

Days later, she, the mistress, wondered if it had been a dream. The plane crash was real enough, headline news. Her pinprick city captured the world's imagination for a brief while because of this "inexplicable" disaster. For years she read the investigative reports, searching through the pages for any mention of what she witnessed. Nothing. Climatic conditions yielded no proof and a light rain was not grounds for lightning. Despite that, she willingly suspended disbelief. A visual spectacle, indelible.

On board a flight from Heathrow to Chek Lap Kok, the arrival announcement awakes her from a dream. Less dream than memory, of the last night spent with her lover, a week before departure. Her eyes are wet, even though she hasn't thought of him in years. Yet his voice is making her cry all over again as if she were still twenty, still in love despite what he says. *I'll pay for the abortion*. The looping memory of their last conversation.

It's 2018. A grey shroud surrounds her city. It's always grey skies now. Landing bump and her cellphone beams. A text from Amber, her granddaughter. *Granny, i m here c u soon! Excited!!* She is happy, of course she is, to be seeing her daughter's child again. Amber grew up in Hong Kong and Canada. Nineteen and a half, an intern at an "international art investment brokerage," whatever that is. Her university studies in visual communications frighten her parents, who believe Amber will never find work. *They were SOOOO wrong, Granny! Tks 4 believing in me.* The text at the start of summer when she landed this plum position, two years before graduation. All she had done was introduce Amber to a friend in the art world and before lightning could strike, there was Amber off to Hong Kong, in business class no less, bunking in her former home. Her daughter June, the social science professor, is flummoxed. She has never been flown in business anywhere by her university. Millennials, her daughter says, they have it all.

Gazing at the wide expanse of the airport from her first class seat — the upgrade arranged by her husband — she reflects, not for the first time, that perhaps she was too austere when raising June. Hong Kong still has everything to offer her granddaughter. June doesn't think so. She and her husband immigrated to Canada when Amber was nine, returning only to visit. Amber Tam *loves* Hong Kong. The New Territories are her "favorite outdoors," unlike the vast Canadian wilderness that intimidates her. She loves the convenience, the public transport, the buzz, all that easy nightlife, the food! Amber loves to eat, and it's a pleasure feeding her. June and her husband, they can take or leave food, jazzed as they are by intellectual, not material pursuits. June's a filial daughter, worries after her even though she really doesn't need to, especially not since her marriage five years earlier. At 65, imagine! To a wellheeled English sculptor ten years her junior with a home in London. Amber thinks Granny is *awesome*. June, she suspects, is still embarrassed.

At arrivals, her granddaughter flies at her in a shrieking embrace. Amber's tall, and she's shrunk. *We look like Mutt and Jeff* and Amber says, *who?*

He had been tall, a visiting professor at her university from Yale's School of Art. Twenty years her senior, a distinguished historian of Chinese and Japanese art, paying her heed. To swoon or not? She swooned. Remembering him now, probably because of Amber, she wants to tell her granddaughter *you look quite a lot like him*. Despite Amber's Cantonese father and June who looks almost all Chinese, virtually erasing the Caucasian blood, this DNA leapfrog gave Amber his cheekbones, his mouth, even that insistent stare that made his eyes glow. Thinking of him now, she is shocked at his callousness, even though back then, she forgave, forgave, forgave him. Why? Because he made her laugh over Mutt and Jeff? Because he followed her to Kowloon City near the airport where no one would see them together? Because her friend Kam owned that great 唐樓, the entire threestory building, and lent them the top floor flat for their trysts? Roaring jets punctuated their sex. Imagining him now, she is shocked at his jokey endearment — "cheap date" — because she didn't crave fancy European restaurants, presenting him instead the best of local cuisine, inexpensive back then. Most of all, she is shocked at the cliché he was, *my wife doesn't understand, doesn't appreciate local culture like me. I could live here forever* with you. *Marry me.* Shocked she was so easily fooled. Family abandoned her. Friends turned their backs. And she? She left university to earn the daily rice bowl. What else could she do? June had no family, only discipline to excel in school, plus her meagre, exhausted maternal love.

Amber's text, three weeks earlier, *Granny I'm in love* and during their Facetime chat, the truth gushed forth. She can picture all: her friend the Berlin art gallery owner invites Amber to *the* party and she's a star — super smart, fashionably attractive, sexual. *Young.* And Amber is in love, or thinks she is, with that brilliant and beautiful Jamaican installation artist visiting from London — *have you heard of him Granny he's really famous* — who promises to take her to Seoul, Singapore, Paris, Barcelona, all those grand cities where *he'll introduce me around.* She is already talking about taking time off from school *it'll be soooo good for my career he loves Hong Kong wants to be here with me…* on and on, gushing, swayed by Granny's twilight romance. Knowing she has Granny's flat, anytime. Dismissing Granny's warnings that the man's too old, that he's in love with her youth and rentfree Hong Kong, that he'll vanish when his yellow fever abates. *That he lies to seduce,* as her almostgrandfather did. She is here, now, trying to shelter Amber from her own exuberant storm. She is here now, waiting again for lightning to strike.

WINTER MOON[37]

YOU play his music, listen to multiple renditions of the songs he wrote. You think you know something because you've played "The Nearness of You" so many times that it flows from your fingertips, improvises, transforms, flies.

It's winter on the South Island which means it's summer in New York and New Jersey, where the man in your life spends his nights and days. You do this distance thing because you've bought a "crib" in New Zealand – even though you're not Kiwi – and the first piece of furniture you install is this very heavy, used upright. Its left front wheel has since fallen off, and the piano has been in a "lock up" – more quaint Kiwi English for the room sealed off from the rest of this getaway house-crib – to rent out in your absence for over two years now. But that's another story in the *yet to come*, as the future articulates in Chinese.

So it's winter on the South Island and you're playing the piano in the green room. You had it painted pale green to match the garden. The painter should have been an artist, as should the gentleman contractor who restored your little villa (more quaint Kwinglish) to its former glory. You say bungalow, I say villa. *Let's call the whole thing off.*

It had been some years since you owned a piano. Having moved your life from Hong Kong to New York to be with the man, you join his family in New Jersey every Christmas as well, and graduations, christenings, birthdays, Thanksgivings.

---

37 **"Winter Moon"** – music & lyrics by Hoagy Carmichael & Harold Adamson

Once, you even went to mass, lapsed Catholics though you both were, with his parents and your visiting mother who were not. It was a good life, a wonderful life. The movies of your childhood and his sound-tracked your America. Because you are American, became American long before this man in your life, except that he *is* the America you ought to have married because it was the one you imagined as a child in Hong Kong. Well, perhaps not quite. Your invisible America was greener, cleaner, larger than a railroad flat in Manhattan. You would have a piano, because there always was one in your life. The American you did marry was a music man so there was a piano, and a drum set, and guitars, and an electronic keyboard, and amplifiers, sound-makers aplenty. Until it all went silent. Marriages do that, go silent I mean, while *the music box plays on*. But that's another story of the *backward view*, as the past articulates in Chinese.

Was Hoagy Carmichael your America? By now you can't be sure because his music is mashed up with the soundtracks of memory. Didn't you *always* know "Stardust" or "Lazy River" or "Two Sleepy People" or, yes! "Heart & Soul" which every ivory-tickler knows from even her tiny-person time? *Hadn't* you seen him in the old black & whites late at night, gabbing with those Yankee voices you didn't entirely understand, from a world glimpsed in the pages of *Life?* Or is this all just imagination because it's winter on the South Island and you're living with this man who can recite lines from "Rear Window," "Casablanca," "Cat on a Hot Tin Roof," and more, who identifies Tinseltown and Americana for you, filling in the knowledge gaps?

That's not quite right. You are not exactly living with this man right now. You're at the top of time and he at almost the other end of the zone stretch across the globe that is Time.

This was pre-Skype, which is less long ago than it sounds. You cannot "see" each other and New Zealand Telecom is outrageously expensive. He lives over there, and you live here in this villa with a garden and a green room with a piano that you play for hours.

That winter, "The Nearness of You" became your song. So did many others from the American Songbook. You tried to have the piano tuned but rural enclaves are seldom visited by tuners. Besides, it sounded good enough for an amateur like you. The music was more than America or him or you. The piano caressed your hands, danced melodies round your head, sang love songs to you.

And then you no longer lived together, because you bought a home, a real home in America, not the playpen of New Zealand. Greener, cleaner, and larger than a New York City railroad flat, although still in New York, though not one you knew existed when you imagined the country from Hong Kong in the little-person era. You bought a piano, a bad buy you later discover, because this console will not hold its tuning. Regret passed soon enough. Nights and days of hand holding and dancing. Consolation in your large and green space up north, where the piano was your constant companion.

You envied your ex-husband's guitar portability, and considered learning a woodwind, even stopped to examine a clarinet once in a secondhand store. But the piano! You can lean into its body, stroke its keys, rise and fall to the rhythms of the pedal. Are you being faithful to the man in your life given this promiscuous flirtation with not one, but two pianos? Oh, his stuff is up north (including a bicycle), and your stuff is in the city. You live together; your stuff is in each other's homes. You both embrace George Carlin's monologue on "Stuff," laugh, even though you've never watched it together. You even get mail in New York City, as you do up north, as you do in New Zealand.

So what is this silence into which you write, into which you stare at a close up of silent keys? This piano of the photograph into which you stare sits in an abandoned space, and, like all abandoned spaces, holds a strange allure. Such spaces worry the memory, imprint themselves on your very self once you've left them behind.

Is it spaces or pianos you leave behind?

The South Island piano is a light-colored wood, like oak, and its action recalls a piano you used to play in another time, another space, on a dead-end street in New England. You sold that one and got a better one that thrummed through you, resonant. And then you sold that one to live for a spell in a Cincinnati apartment complex where a swimming pool was its most desirable feature. It would be a long time before another upright entered your life and when it did, the musician was abandoned, along with his guitars and amplifiers and drum set and the electric keyboard in Singapore on which you practiced "La Vie En Rose," a song he never heard you play.

These are years, mind you, we're discussing here. Decades. These are not the passing flirtations of youth.

You time-trip into now and find you cannot abandon Mother. She is old. She cannot remember. Instead, you abandon the hopeless piano that will not hold its tuning in Northern New York. You rent out the South Island crib to strangers whom you never meet. You do all this in order to come "home" to stay till Mother is silenced forever. The pianos sit silent.

And now you really do *not* live with the man in your life

in the upside-down time zone and you sleep when he wakes and wake when he sleeps.

For a brief while, when abandonment was less certain, you spent half a year in the middle of America in a rented space. The house was large and historic and in the garage was an abandoned piano, wedged amid the detritus of a household. You opened its lid, tickled it awake, but it was a little far gone. Besides, it was heavy and immovable and this was the dead of winter. But desire smoldered.

At the music store you tested the weighted keys of an electric keyboard and brought that to your space.

This was when you still lived in almost the same time zone with the man in your life. He was supposed to visit you in the cornfields of Iowa where you settled for a brief spell but Manhattan held him bondage. He never saw Middle America after all, and still has not, this American lover of yours. You write about being American to articulate what it is you have become, to understand how you must eventually live and love.

At the University of Iowa, the library had a section of music scores. You found Hoagy's song book and in it, the anthem for the next years of your life (although you did not know it then). When your brother the composer visited, you played it for him. *Listen,* you said, *I think this was Hoagy's heart.* Your brother the church musician does not always share your taste in music, but this time, he asked for a copy of the score for "Winter Moon" and you made it for him, gladly.

"The American dream," Carlin said, "you have to be asleep to believe it."

In the little-person time, you dreamed yourself into an America of desire, to escape the Hong Kong prison into which you were born, where your voice felt continually silenced. Now, back in this birth city you previously abandoned to be with the man in your life, you install not one, but two electronic keyboards. The multiple soundtracks – *vox humana*, every instrument of the big band and orchestra, sound effects – sit beside your bed. The weighted keys sit in your writing space. The simulation that feels almost like a real piano switches on, comes alive, holds your hand, caresses your heart.

The man in your life is on Skype when schedules mesh.

And you? You listen to Hoagy sing "Winter Moon." You play his songs. You sing the lines to his chord changes.

The other night at some dinner karaoke, a woman selected "The Sound of Silence" and the audience sang along. Time journeys, nostalgia for youth.

And you. You wait, like a winter moon, for summer's return.

JAZZ WIFE

YOU *marry the music not the man.*
Here's that intro no one sings. The old familiars stick to form — AABA, AABA, AABA, AABA. Here's the one to the B that goes *ba-doinnnng,* all wrong.

She walks into that bar, that club, that jazz space and listens to the boys in the band. Comes to visit a bartender, is all.

1978. Jazz is dying in America faster than a doornail that *tings!*

Break.

Trumpet arrives first. Bandleader. Having scoped her out from onstage, he plants himself on her left. "So, you like jazz?"

"Doesn't everyone?" she replies.

"You like musicians?" He's a stand-up comic in his spare time.

Now she swings 'round and scopes him out. *Not* her type, although if you ask, she'll say she has no type. Not at twenty-two, she doesn't. Sips her Scotch and soda. "Don't know."

In the empty room, an elderly couple asks loudly, above their hearing, for "String of Pearls." Pianist appears, singing, *Glenn's dead, forever.* He's Black and White, like she's Black and Yellow. Oreo and banana crumble.

Pianist tells the trumpet, "I'm blowing this gig, man. Screw the money."

"Hey pal. You promised."

"Didn't promise nothin'." His volume rises, pounding the lower register.

She slides off the barstool. *Inconsiderate bastards. Least they could do is take their anger elsewhere.*

Time she left anyway.

The pianist storms out behind her. Tall, skinny, straight ahead. Even mad, he's looking good. His car, blocking hers, doesn't start, here in the middle of — *fucking nowhere,* he shouts — into the still of the night.

You don't sing in the shower, or anywhere, unless you have perfect pitch.

At her place around an ancient upright, she sings, *Someday, when I'm awfully low.*

"You're flat," he says.

"So how do I hear better?"

"You listen. Maybe tape yourself."

She plays the opening to "Misty," the only standard she knows.

He interrupts. "Your rhythm's off."

"Rubato," she replies.

"Wise guy."

"I ain't a guy," and stops playing to prove it.

But when he plays, she falls in love with the miracle of his touch, the sprawl of his octaves, the grace of his ballads, and the speed of his bebop. The man can play. He's still a boy, though, like she's still a girl, when he finally stops playing to kiss her.

They live together in Cincinnati.

Time is a half note, a quarter note, an eighth, a sixteenth.

"Demisemiquaver?" she asks, recalling foreign music theory. "Crochets and semibreves?"

He spits back jazz. "Modes," he says. "Dorian, lydian. Modal like Bill Evans, or crazy like Powell and Tristano."

"Paganini was a wild man, like Dad." The story of her life is the accident of conception, in Hong Kong, between a Black American banjo player and a Chinese stripper in the bars of Wanchai. She, an immigrant daughter in her father's hometown, searches for roots, writes about Paganini to get, belatedly, a bachelor's degree in something.

"*I'll* teach you about music," he says. "But first you have to marry me."

"I'm not a musician," she replies.

"You could be if you tried."

But she's not sure, has never been sure, whether or not to believe him.

To-*may*-to, to-*ma*-to. *Let's call the whole thing off.*

You learn to feed the boys in the band.

Running out the door of their marriage in Cincinnati, he shouts up the stairs, "We're rehearsing at eight."

Their home in Clifton is old and rambling. Ivy clings. Hours spent scrubbing and vacuuming because he cannot abide the tiniest speck.

Today, though, she doesn't clean. When the guys rehearse, the aftermath is like a bar the morning after. Bass player smokes, drummer inhales. The front line rotates, depending on availability — trumpet, trombone, tenor, alto, flute — and, because tonight he's really desperate, the oboe. Too many bottles of beer. Empties line the wall of his studio.

They're guys now. Boys belonged to a quainter era.

What she does instead is season the *wok* to prepare for their midnight feast. *Don't ask, just cook.* Collard greens for the Black players, nothing too weird for the Whites. Yellow doesn't play, not in Cincinnati. When they smell it they break. This way he eats, keeps up strength for the next gig and the next, if and when one comes along.

Afterwards, the complaints. Trumpet too loud, bass doesn't swing, and there are *way too many reasons* an oboe does not belong in jazz. The oboist, a blond from the college orchestra, needs rides all the time — which he gives — because her car keeps breaking down. The one girl in the band. *Why doesn't she change her axe,* he groans.

But to change your axe is to change your life.

"Are oboes like trumpets?" she asks.

He snaps. "How would I know?"

Why is he angry? She only meant to make him laugh with that joke among the guys. About the trumpet player at the club, that gal with the mouth. A jazz wife in the audience doesn't count, except to listen to the path of his solos.

They don't have sex after rehearsals.

In time, the oboe moves on and he makes love to her again.

It's the gigs you miss most. The real jazz gigs.

Sometimes, a cat blows in from New York. If he's lucky, it's not a piano man. Then he's in demand. Everyone needs rhythm.

Guys have become men.

A first-call jazz man. Blows his regular lounge gigs for these. Anything for a chance to play the real thing.

She is thirty. "I'm getting up there," she says. "Fertility's dying."

"Later," he murmurs his refrain. Sometimes, he forgets he has this wife, the girl to whom he once played "My Romance."

If it isn't music, it's later.

Yet every time he pounds a fist she flinches, afraid *only* for his hands, those precious, life-making hands.

But at the club that night, the real gig night, jazz wives congregate. Tonight, they're out catting. Silk stockings for New York, and even Chicago, but not L.A.

They know *everyone's* song.

On the bandstand, he's in a suit, out of respect, regardless. Tonight, New York is white and young in jeans, barely out of boyhood. A genius on tenor.

She is proud. The music is all.

Not a cough in the house, the half empty house.

You get and keep steady work.

"So what're you doing this weekend?" her bachelor colleague has asked every Friday afternoon for over six months.

"Oh you know," she smiles. "Same old same old. He's working."

"Don't you go to all his gigs?"

"Not anymore."

Guys hover. Black and Yellow is exotic in Ohio. This one has thin lips and sexy gray eyes. Wait, she thinks, *are* gray eyes sexy? He's nice, though, asks about her, not him, her nearly famous husband, at least in Cincinnati.

Her colleague says, "Don't you get jealous of all those singers?" By now, her husband's a first-call accompanist in fancy lounges, as far north as Chicago, where he's playing this week.

"He's not like that," she replies. "He comes home." The oboe, she has surmised, was an aberration. In his book, the *only* singers are Billie and Betty.

"You're in love," he says, as he does every time, the standard bridge to eyes that invite, *anytime you're tired of being a good wife.*

Music is the wife.
AABA, AABA, AABA, AA *ba-doinnnng.*

Until she becomes famous for a day.

One Saturday evening, she rescues a child. He breaks away from pregnant Mom and runs headlong into traffic. Blind instinct sends her after the boy, pulling him to safety. The driver brakes hard. Cars collide. A total mess.

All she can remember, as she tells the TV cameras, is the boy's face looking up at her. Trusting, unafraid. Confident in his innocence, a belief in his right to life.

The Cincinnati Enquirer sends their newest hire. He waits till after the cameras depart, annoyed. It's his thirtieth birthday and drinks are on his friends.

In a nearby bar, they talk for over an hour. He catches himself asking more and more questions, long after the story, just to keep the conversation going. He eyes her legs, reminds himself, *this is work, she is married, I am… a man.* Afterwards, she thanks him for the drink, pausing to notice gray eyes and a mouth like her colleague's.

The headline reads: JAZZ WIFE SAVES CHILD.
Crescendo.
Music pauses.

In time, the reporter moves on. Larger city, bigger paper. To write about music. She's been a good teacher, in and out of bed, elevating him beyond the news.

Jazz wife gives life. Her husband is none the sadder.

Time after time. So lucky to be loving you.
The passing years unfold, childless.

The night he plays "Nature Boy," she goes, uninvited, unexpected.

From onstage, he sees her arrive. Doesn't smile, doesn't break into "Our Romance" the way he used to, years ago, whenever she came to a gig among friends.

His solo begins.

The best performance of his life. It's in his face. His eyes gaze past all to music heaven. The boys in the band play hard, for him, with him, in him, caught up in the frenzy, in this, his moment of genius. In the empty house, she hears it too, feels his solitary flight.

Then, his face becomes one with that child. Trusting. Unafraid. Certain of his right to be saved, to survive. In her solitude, she knows. If it hadn't been her it would have been somebody else.

She leaves, at last, in the middle of his solo.

After he's gone, you live for the music.

I HAD A "TIGER MOM"[38] AND MY LOVE FOR HER IS Ω

Tyger, tyger burning bright, etc. – William Blake[39]

I HAD a tiger mom. She was Chinese but really a *wah kiu,* an "overseas Chinese," meaning she no longer lived on the mainland, inside the great wall. A funny thing, that. The safety of the wall means you can no longer rely simply on the *wah,* the Chinese-ness that is unquestionably superior to the rest of the world, if you call yourself Chinese and are a tiger mom, that is. That's what China — 中國— *really* means, you know – the center that presides over the universe. *Superior.* Like shark's fin or bird's nest or other delicacies in superior XO sauce in expensive restaurants that offer up false cuisines, dingy toilets, and surly, underpaid wait staff. Of course that's also why the Qing Dynasty collapsed and China was in chaos for decades afterwards, and is still chaotic today, but we skip over the facts in favor of what we prefer to believe. Contributes to more robust tigress-ness, oblivious to the possibility that Chinese-ness can also embrace cleanliness, a

---

38 *Battle Hymn of the Tiger Mother* by Amy Chua (2011) is a book more hyped than essential. Its greatest contribution to modern culture, in this writer's view, is the absurdity of pretending to be ironic when, in fact, the author, like most authors, is actually *deathly* serious about her superior perspective on parenting, Chinese style. Why else write a book, or anything, after all, if you are not holier than thou, a greater know-it-all than the next know-it-all, or someone who thinks she has more to say than most and wants the world to pay you a shitload of cash for the privilege of being touched by your words, or at least remembered for your words, as all poets and writers believe (till death proves otherwise) is their due? Present company not excepted.

39 William Blake (1757-1827) is the dead poet who, having been canonized, at least by the Anglo-Americans and their English language, is studied in English by Chinese schoolchildren unfortunate enough to have been born and raised in a former British colony, thereby contributing to aspirations of poesy and scribbling long after such poems as his "The Tyger" would otherwise be relegated to the recesses of oblivion, Lethe-wards sunk. Wasn't *he* privileged? We who 'write back' from the former Empire exact revenge; vengeance is, of course, never gracious.

reasonable existence, and tolerance and respect for family and other intimates. Include yourself.

I had a tiger mom once. She was mostly Chinese but there were droplets of Indonesian blood infused from the five generations her family had inhabited Central Java. She seldom mentioned that blood, except to brag when we, my three siblings and I, were children, of its royal origins (Balinese princess, she said). Tigresses must be pure-blooded, or else, noble savages. None of the civilized, domesticated pussycat variety. No ma'am.

I had a Chinese tiger mom, since these days we hear there are Indian ones[40] as well (and no doubt a host of others on that same bandwagon). She spoke Javanese with native fluency, studied English in Singapore, and remained virtually illiterate in Chinese because she found the characters too difficult to memorize under tropical skies. Yet there we were, her children in Hong Kong, poring over the language she herself failed to love. The shame (*oh, for shame!*) of her fake Chinese-ness was too great and if she could fix her children she would. A fearful symmetry is like that, in the forest of the long night that is motherhood in a foreign, Chinese-tainted-by-the-British land.[41] That my Chinese today is better than hers ever was is probably something she'd rather forget. Has forgotten.

I have a tiger mom who, at 92, is not yet past tense, although her memory is, lost to Alzheimer's. Funny what she does

---

40 *The Wall Street Journal,* or some other such "authoritative source" reported that and the best way to undermine authority is simply not to recall the details of its power source, especially as such mass produced, glib twitters across the globe are merely technology's litter.

41 As compared to her familiar Chinese-tainted-by-Indonesian-but-thank-goodness-the-Dutch-are-gone homeland. In the end, it doesn't much matter what kind of Chinese you are if you're home, a space that still eludes me, as I sashay ever further away from the borders of middle age.

recall. The occasional Cantonese phrase pops out, although sometimes she speaks to me in Javanese, a language she never taught us. When we pass the Chinese signs on buildings in Kowloon (we rarely cross the harbor to the island of Hong Kong anymore except to see her doctor), she will sometimes read them aloud. 新年 new year; 學校 school; 銀行 bank[42]. Although she spoke "run-tune,"[43] incomprehensibly accented Cantonese during her Hong Kong life, some Mandarin bits, which she studied as a child in Indonesia, creep in. Tiger mom-ness clings fiercely to its Chinese-ness, despite all her condemnation of Confucius as "old fashioned" and "outdated" when we were children. Confucius, the indisputably Chinese scholar she never read. The one I did read and think of as a dragon king with spectacles. Mythic, casting long shadows, forcing you to continually investigate, even now in the 21st century, what it means to be Chinese, something my tiger mom never did, convinced as she was that merely being was all it took.

Tiger mom, my love for her is… but I am not yet ready to say it. First I must tell you how fiercely she raised me to succeed.

---

42 Traditional or "complicated" Chinese characters because, despite China's Rise -- a phrase if googled yields far too many echoes – we Chinese in Hong Kong still preserve the sanctity of the traditional language, with all its impossible radicals and strokes, a written language which contributes to the most privileged Chinese (*Good, better best / Let us never rest / Till our good is better / And our better best* – from a remembered childhood English work book, *Word Perfect*, I believe, published by, who else, the Americans?), anyway, the most privileged Chinese children on the globe today (i.e. mainland *nouveau riche* and the offspring of the cadres) being thankful for the simplified version popularized by Deng Xiaoping who failed to discern any notable difference between a black or white cat whose function, after all, is merely to catch mice, or so he quipped. Deng failed to reckon with tiger moms or their descendants who will no doubt seek the most strenuous Sisyphean path possible to achieving superior Chinese literacy, playing an instrument or excelling in any discipline, regardless of its futility to a life of reason.

43 走音 literally the running or slippery tune or tone where even the slightest tonal shift changes meaning profoundly or may be misconstrued, as in 馬 (horse) for 媽 (mother), both of the first tone 'MA', at least in Mandarin cum Putonghua. Cantonese is yet another tonal dilemma.

It is incumbent upon offspring of tigresses to document that
stellar upbringing. How did she raise me? Let me count the
ways. Linguistically confused. Culturally uncertain. Bound
and determined to succeed in that which was not my forte
(*physicist, doctor, capitalist chief*) until I finally said *enough, no,
you may be my mother but I am no longer a tiger cub.* For one
thing, I discovered I might be a pussycat, or possibly even a
mutt, entirely of the wrong species. More correctly, I probably
belonged to the gorilla or chimpanzee Mum; they groom
their young and make loud, smacking, disgusting sounds of
affection.

My tiger mom, loving her is manifest, strangely, in a love of
music, for which I have some, though not significant, talent.
My mother learned to play "The Blue Danube"[44] on the piano
by heart, or so we were told all through our childhood, when
each of us was made to learn an instrument. Notably, we
never heard her performance of same. I stuck out the piano,
passed exams moderately well, performed regularly on stage to
minimal acclaim, a feat she never even witnessed. The problem
was, the problem still is, is that she's tone-deaf. Why it was
such a necessary accomplishment to memorize and play some
abridged child's version of a pop tune by Strauss is lost to the
recesses of tiger memory.

When Alzheimer's first was manifest, after Dad's death
and before we fully understood its impact, I used to fly back
from New York frequently for my writing life. Tiger Mom,
being still in charge then, said, *stay here,* meaning at home,
because tiger cubs must be close to their mother. I shrugged,
agreed, even though it was a bad idea, because it was cheaper,

---

44 My mother could have saved herself the agony and tears it must have cost her to
memorize the score and force her fingers to eke out the tune if only she'd been born
a century later, when www.youcanplayit.com could have done it for her on YouTube.
Personally, I preferred "The Emperor's Waltz."

and I had left the security of corporate life for the uncertainty of art. I bought an inexpensive electronic keyboard, because I have always played for pleasure, but home was now (is still) in the U.S. and I no longer owned a piano or home in Hong Kong. She watched, glared, as the keyboard took up its tiny amount of space. Wanted to cover it, wanted to move it, wanted to, basically, kick up a fuss about it. Destroy it. We, my Hong Kong sister and I, puzzled over her distress.

Later, we said, *the Alzheimer's,* as surely that was it. But sometimes I think, now that reason no longer matters, was it the conflict of wanting to excel in what she really couldn't that made her so angry, so hateful, that her daughter could play piano but not tennis, the thing my mother truly excelled at? Does a tiger mom most wish to reproduce clones, to excel in her image, to live the life she couldn't because she was too busy being mother instead of the successful – doctor / tennis star / clan chieftain because Chinese fathers, while perhaps not tigers, are nonetheless dictatorial chiefs of at least their immediate clan[45] – opting instead for tigress-ness, ferocity masking wounded pride? That was a too-long sentence but reflections on my tiger mom give rise to convoluted thought.

I moved the piano out of her line of sight, and memory. *Burning bright.* The jumble of thwarted recall.

---

45 This is a known fact. Ask any Chinese.

Tiger mom, my love for her is . . . but "All The Way"[46] gets in
the way, the tune that begins:

When somebody loves you. Troubling, though, is that it is the
bridge, and not the opening, that echoes: *Deeper than the deep
blue sea is / That's how deep it goes if it's real.*[47]

She screamed at me once, *I disown you,* because I had "run
away with the family fortune," or so sister number three told
me. We had no family fortune – unless you count the change
my father left in his wardrobe, coins neatly separated for bus
fare – but Dad's business had finally improved and he gave me
a down payment to purchase a small starter home in the U.S.
Now it belonged to me and my new husband and therein lies
the rub. Dad put our final family home (a 1200-square-foot
flat) in only my mother's name, because his earlier bankruptcy
had shamed him into defeat. I am daughter number one, child

---

46 "All the Way" (1957) music by Jimmy Van Heusen, lyrics by Sammy Cahn,
received the best original song Academy Award in that same year. A good thing, too,
because it subsequently got covered by numerous artistes, most popularly by Frank
Sinatra, but it was thanks to some unremarkable version by either Ray Conniff & his
singers or someone similar – I don't quite remember – which I first heard, learned
and memorized as an unduly romantic teen in Hong Kong of the '60s. Infatuated
dreaming is like that when you're young, and then some things stick, forcing their
way forth at the most inconvenient times, like when you're essaying on the meaning
of love for your tiger mother. Unfortunately now there is google so you can *almost*
track down everything you once recalled, unlike my mother, who cannot research,
never mind recall, what she had for breakfast five minutes after she's eaten. What
good is life that goes all this way (she might live to 100; her even more Alzheimer-
ridden elder sister lived to 99)? Is it any good if life stops loving you, i.e.: your memory
goes *widdershins,* and then life is merely the minute-to-minute, second-to-second
existence where every breath you take / every move you make / every step you take,
etc. denies you were ever once a thinking, cognitive, interactive-with-the-human-race
soul? And that was Sting, of course, and The Police, but you know that because you're
cognitive now, and not in 1957, which is in your grandmother's memory, maybe.

47 Lyrics, mind you, root themselves in the hippocampus in ways that even poems by
the highly canonized do not. I had to look up "The Tyger" to recall all the lines, but
recalled, almost 100% correctly, the song lyrics to "All the Way" which, two lines before
the end, go: *Who knows where the road will lead us / Only a fool would say.* Lyricists,
although also writers, might not take themselves as seriously as those so-called "real"
poets & writers, which is why they manage to be wiser and more memorable, unafraid
as they are of the basic tenets of life, the things clever editors would term clichés.
When I grow old, I may not wear my trousers rolled, but I want to keep hearing the
songbook, regardless of Alzheimer's, should misfortune prove *that* hereditary.

number one, for years her Daddy's girl. A bad thing to be when tiger mom reigns, and worse if you marry a music man, the one who was most like Dad, right down to their horoscope sign.

Was it deep, was it real, the love she claimed she had for me, for all her children?

This is the most difficult question to answer because now, I can no longer ask her. Her speech is impaired by Alzheimer's and she forms words with difficulty, especially in the afternoons and evenings. Night arrives earlier and earlier because her eyesight is blurred by cataracts; the operation to remove them was one she refused and refused and refused to do, and then one day, her memory was gone – *widdershins* – and we could no longer persuade her to consider it. She is also partially deaf, ever since she secretly discarded the hearing aid my sister purchased for *not* a song, oh a decade or so ago, except that is, perhaps, a mercy. Because now she no longer needs to be assaulted by the cacophony that music must be to her, all that opera Daddy loved and used to spin on his phonograph, all the piano I once played at home, even the hymns sung at her Catholic church, religion still being her blessed refuge, even now for this lost lamb. All that music she was forced to revere but never really loved.

Daddy sang, played violin. Daddy wasn't tone-deaf, like her, and he never answered this question that hovered, unasked, between us. But I knew he knew I wanted to know and sometimes I want to ask – *did she love me* – but even now, when he is only an imaginary, rooting around in some consciousness I cannot completely control, I cannot form the words. Instead, the dragon king lowers his spectacles, peers over the rim, rhetoricizes, *now why do you, a Chinese, need to ask this?* To be filial is all. To be dutiful to Tiger Mom in her dotage. To groom her now as she once groomed you, the cub, pussycat, baby pup or chimp. What difference does love make? *What a difference a day makes,*[48] croons the perennial optimist. What difference does love make when all that's left is the skin of the tiger, almost a rug, inanimate?

Tyger, tyger, tyger mom, do I "love" her because I live at home now, squatting on her rooftop, helping to manage her Alzheimer's care? *Haau seon,*[49] filial, the definition of being Chinese you cannot escape from. My Hong Kong sister and I look at each other – *do we believe we're doing this?* – we two eldest girls who were the most rebellious, the most troublesome, the least dutiful or loving daughters. We *tygers.*

In the flat below that once was our family's home my mother fumbles through her days. Sundowner's syndrome, which affects patients with Alzheimer's, is a daily ritual. Darkness arrives, earlier and earlier because when the sun is overhead, the east facing flat no longer glows with the overly bright glare of morning sunshine; by afternoon, her senses say it is night. As darkness arrives, even in the mornings, because our city lives under a gloomy haze of pollution too often now, she must wonder what happened to daylight, to all her days.

The ritual – and being Chinese, especially Confucian, is all about ritual – is the curtains. The floor-to-ceiling accordion glass doors that lead to the verandah must be pulled shut, regardless of either heat or chill because she no longer feels the

---

48 Originally, "Cuando Vuelva A Tu Lado" by Mexican composer María Méndez Grever (1934) and adapted and recorded, later that same year, into English with lyrics by Stanley Adams as "What a Diff'rence a Day Makes." The original song title actually means "when I return to your side," which shifts the point of view to the first person, to the one responsible for taking action to make the so-called "diff'rence." If I return to my mother's side it makes a difference to her day, or at least to the moment of that day when she is cognizant of my presence. But that passes, in far less than the "twenty-four little hours" of the American song lyrics, amid the ADHD that is Alzheimer's (and here I mix, not metaphors, but classifications of the DSM, the Diagnostic & Statistical Manual of Mental Disorders, which is chock full of language to horrify the soul that searches for either enlightenment or peace).

49 孝順

difference anyway. She closes the long, yellow-gold curtains, searches around for a clip to secure their edges in the middle. Shuts out the world. It can happen at mid afternoon or early evening, although I have come into her flat in the mornings to find the curtains closed. The two domestic helpers, who live with her and provide 24-7 watchfulness, are used to this by now. *Mama*, they say, having become her new tiger cubs, *Mama closed the curtains because it's nighttime.* They are Filipino, younger than any of us, these women who have become my mother's good girls who never answer back, always agree with her, say whatever she wants to hear, as they've been instructed to do.

A few days ago, I sat with my mother at her dining table. *I have so much to do,* she told me, to which I replied, *yes, you do.* There was the clip for the curtains she had to buy, the things at home she had to go through, *the, the, the,* and if she could say it, she'd say, *the life I once had.* And then her gaze panned to the cut flowers in the vase, flowers the helpers replenish weekly in imitation of the ritual of my childhood when my mother regularly brought home an armful of flowers from the market and made gorgeous arrangements for our home. Until recently, she could still name the carnation, gladiola, lily, orchid, daisy, although she puzzled over some of the hybrids and their startlingly unnatural shapes and colors, these false blooms beyond her ken. False nature, as false as her Alzheimer's days, as false as the Chinese-ness she embraced and eschewed, as false as the Tiger Mom who was only trying to love her family, a love that the linguistically and culturally confused world of her life made more difficult than it needed to be.

Or was it? Do I mis-remember because it is the kinder thing to do now, the *filial* thing? To give up on the anger and hatred and rage of being bred in the tiger's lair? You have chosen not to procreate, knowing that your role model was too fierce, too willful, too painful, too, too, too, to replicate. And yet, wasn't it she who gave you the small things that offer solace as you steal your own way towards twilight? A love for nature. Food prepared fresh, by your own hand, in all its natural simplicity. A determination to endure.

I had a tiger mom and my love for her cannot be named. Love is the province of poets and writers who are fool enough to try to name the unsayable. It has less to do with how Chinese I am than how singular the experience of not being able to utter love for my mother feels. You cannot go around saying – *I do not love my mother* – although you have tried. You cannot complain and complain and complain about your lot in life because even you tire of it, never mind those around you. You cannot lull yourself into that fatalistic female drumbeat – *no choice, no choice, what choice do I have?* – when feminist foremothers fought for your freedom of choice. You cannot even resort to your late aunt's favorite phrase –*no use don't ask* – an utterance to shut up and out the inexplicable.

Instead you can write, *I had a tiger mom and my love for her is,* and, instead of inserting a comma or ellipsis or some misguided word or even song lyric, you can end the sentence, unfinished.

Ω **The endnote** (or End-note)

The first known use of the endnote, according to Merriam-Webster's Unabridged, was in 1926. Merriam-Webster does not have more to say about said usage beyond this, which begs the question of the inclusion of such a fact. In fact, "nonfiction" as a literary genre begs the question of its nonfictional attribution. Is it nonfiction as opposed to factual or is it the negation of fiction? Why is it even termed "nonfiction" and not more descriptively named memoir, travel writing, literary journalism, *et al*, or any of the various genres or sub-genres that "nonfiction" assumes? A more precise name for at least the short form is, quite simply, the essay.

In such a mind did I set out to write this endnote for my footnoted essay "I Had a Tiger Mom and My Love for Her Is." Footnoting is not a format normally favored by the journal *TEXT*, in which this work appears. I like footnotes, especially when they provide more than mere reference, especially when they extend the authorial perspective and tone, especially when they become a space for creative, satirical, or informational articulation for this increasingly popular literary genre "nonfiction." The late David Foster Wallace used footnotes for literary effect as for example in his essay collection *Consider the Lobster*, which was factual but also creatively nonfictional. It was possible to learn more than most readers, or indeed even the writer himself, would need or wish to know about the lobster from the title essay, and yet the piece was as entertaining and compelling as a good yarn in fiction. CNF, as creative nonfiction is shorthanded, is the name for a kind of writing that is a catch all for much that is literary today which cannot easily be classified as either "poetry" or "fiction."

Just how did contemporary writing arrive at this state?

Before I contemplate the question, it is worth noting that the Oxford English Dictionary only chose to add the noun "endnote" in 1993, hyphenated, claiming its origins to be in the U.S.A. One click away is the non-synonym, the footnote (at least it appears to be dubiously synonymous), which, for this avid reader of dictionaries, led to an 1864 reader's comment on same, to wit, *The result of all this footnoting and appendix-*

noting, is that the volume has a most chaotic and bewildering look.
Chaos, however, is the character of our age as the inexhaustible
data cornucopia wifi-ies its way 24/7 across the planet with
or without the assistance of Edgar Snowden; Snowden may
eventually be forgotten unless properly footnoted for history
(or confused with his almost namesake Lord Snowdon, *a.k.a.*
Anthony Armstrong-Jones, who achieved a comparable
notoriety, both these men of slippery positions in the world).
Perhaps the footnote deserves reconsideration, deserves
elevation to a more exalted role as a form of literary expression?
In fiction, Junot Diaz used the footnote as a history lesson,
among other things, in his Pulitzer Prize-winning novel *The
Brief Wondrous Life of Oscar Wao.* It was his way to contextualize
the otherwise little-known history of the Dominican Republic
against which the protagonist and narrative needed to be read.

Or should we trust the willingness of the reader to look up the
facts in order to read the fiction or essay?

As a student of English and American literature back in my
undergraduate days at a New York state university, it was
assumed that I would learn both nations' histories in tandem
with their literature. That was in the early 1970s, when the
canon was relatively sacred and an educated reader could be
expected to know her Donne and Dickens, or distinguish
between the two Eliots, or recognize that a novel was fiction
(unlike the "nonfiction novel" which now appears to be its own
genre) while *A Modest Proposal* was satire rooted in a form of
creative nonfiction, even if we didn't call it that back then. At
the dawn of the 21st century, Nonfiction Now! assumes the
urgency of exclamation, at least in the conference logo bearing
that name, and "text" has morphed into something that is
divorced from literature in the English language as it once was
writ (perhaps it was never a good marriage). Not only did the

Empire "write back," as the 1989 nonfiction book by Ashcroft, Griffiths and Tiffin on post-colonial literature claimed, the rest of the world decided that English, or something akin, would become its *lingua franca* for this moment of history. Which meant the language would absorb much more than European terms like *cul de sac* or *bildungsroman*. Suddenly, sushi, wifi, Putonghua, tiger mom, Gangnam style, Facebook, yin-yang, 7-11, 9-11, 2.0, or OS X became recognizably "English" terms, just as tweet as verb or Twitter as proper noun took on brandly new meanings. Even "brand" expanded beyond a verb to describe the presumably painful act of stamping ownership on a herd of cattle. In fact, if not for the brand-consulting firm Interbrand Corporation, we might still be writing IEEE 802.11b Direct Sequence instead of the term wifi. Look it up, Wikipedia knows more than The Shadow these days (even if radio is not dead, radio plays no longer have the importance they had back when Shadow was a proper noun), and if it's in Wikipedia it must be fact, right?

Nonfiction now is all about too many facts (we could discuss the aside as well but this endnote on footnotes is already sufficiently chaotic without courting further bewilderment). Facts imply some brand of knowledge which in turn prompts an authorial perspective that attempts to digest these myriad facts, factoids, and maybe-facts in order to write an essay about one's mother with Alzheimer's. Alzheimer's is all about too little memory for too many facts, so that the latter becomes jumbled into a non-timeline of fictional and nonfictional memory. Yet memory itself, the one thing for sure that any personal essayist calls upon, is about as reliable as the English language that morphs and transforms at the speed of wifi. Add to that 4000-plus years of Chinese history, culture, and language that has not only morphed into the Communist Party, tiger moms, and Putonghua in pinyin, all of which shaped this particular writer's worldview (as well as her mother's)… well, where *do* you begin to tell the story? *Where do I begin / To tell the story of how great a love can be?* Or not, as the case may be? Did I remember to add that writing about a tone deaf mother who must negotiate a tonal language, especially when music is in your blood, can and will give rise to the 'unheard melodies' Keats found sweeter? Those lines of lyrics are from the opening of the song 'Love Story,' composed by the French accordionist and composer Francis Lai with lyrics by Carl Sigman and originally published in 1970. Yet as the song was widely popularized by the American vocalist Andy Williams, the lyrics are sometimes wrongly attributed to him. Look it up. Google it. If Google says so it must be fact, right?

This endnote ought to have footnotes but in a desire not to further add to the chaos and bewilderment of this essayistic endnote that refuses to be academic despite its critical nature, I will refrain. The other truth, universally or otherwise acknowledged, is that nonfiction now has pushed beyond traditional academic boundaries, offering knowledge in new and even startling forms. The lyric essay, for instance, that looks like a poem, feels like a poem but is maybe more than only a poem, such as Ann Carson's "The Glass Essay" which is located in both an anthology of essays (John D'Agata's *The Next American Essay)* as well as in the archives of The Poetry Foundation. David Shields's *Reality Hunger: A Manifesto,* a significant work in the debate about contemporary writing, is the ultimate list essay where factual attribution is deliberately obfuscated. Despite Shields's pronouncements that fiction has died yet again, his own work skirts the edges of NON-fiction that could be read as more fictional than not. In *The Lifespan of a Fact,* John D'Agata provokes us to reflect on the meaning of fact in his partly fictional correspondence with Jim Fingal, the former fact checker for the journal *The Believer.* Ripley's

Believe It or Not, the cartoon strip I read religiously through my childhood in Hong Kong, feels oddly relevant.

We can no longer be too literal about text, even though literal-ness remains a distinct and markedly Hong Kong trait, something to be noted if you must live in the city where your mother faces fear each sundown of her lost remembrances. There is something about absorbing English as a language in this post-colonial, pre-mainland- Chinese city that invites literal meanings to things (there is a future shock footnote about the year – and indie film – 2046 in this naming of Hong Kong as pre-mainland Chinese but perhaps, unlike Diaz, I might trust the reader to look up the facts?). Nury Vittachi, the Sri Lankan-Hong Kong author and humorist, has often noted in his work that the city's buildings have markedly literal names, for example, the building named "Skyscraper." It feels safe, perhaps, to eat at "Quite Good Noodles Restaurant" (a literal translation of its Chinese name) or for a waitress to sport a badge reading "Waitress." Vittachi doesn't say why this must be so, just that it is so, which is much of what nonfiction now has become, to record and capture the reality we are so hungry for, if Shields is to be believed. When we opine, we lean towards outrage, even favoring deliberate diversion or digression, in order to generate another layer of text upon text, the way a footnote can if not read too literally. In the personal essay where emotions are at risk – the investigation of whether or not you truly 'love' your mother, say – this layering effect can be comforting, a 'face blanket' like the one Linus carries, in order not to lose face, this Chinese cultural avoidance tactic that a Chinese-Indonesian-American writer from and of Hong Kong owns as part of her DNA, whether she admits to it or not. To echo the essay (or CNF piece) that precedes this endnote, that was a too-long sentence but reflections on the meaning of footnotes as creative text vs. reference source (on account of the editorial bewilderment of the readers for the journal *TEXT*) give rise to convoluted thought.

On that note, the end, as all fictions, once earnestly begun, must end.

CPSIA information can be obtained
at www.ICGtesting.com
Printed in the USA
BVHW052039120623
665833BV00008B/195

9 781915 531001